DEATH ON THE LINE

Maggie tried to stop me. "Miss Agnes," she beseeched. "Go to bed and don't listen. Don't answer the telephone. It's nothing human that rings that bell."

But I was determined to conquer my fear. I went downstairs to the rear hall, that cul-de-sac of nervousness in the daytime and horror at night, and took up my vigil beside the telephone.

The fear welled up like a flood, and swept me with it. I wanted to shriek. I was afraid to shriek. I longed to escape, I dared not move. I sat with fixed eyes, not even blinking, for fear of even for a second shutting out the sane and visible world about me.

Then the telephone bell rang. Somehow I reached forward and took down the receiver.

"Who is it?" I cried.

There was complete silence. The circuit had been stealthily cut.

Contents

The Confession

Chapter 1

I am not a susceptible woman. I am objective rather than subjective, and a fairly full experience of life has taught me that most of my impressions are from within out, rather than the other way. For instance, obsession at one time a few years ago of a shadowy figure on my right, just beyond the field of vision, was later exposed as the result of a defect in my glasses. In the same way Maggie, my old servant, was during one entire summer haunted by church bells and considered it a personal summons to eternity until it was shown to be in her inner ear.

Yet the Benton house undeniably made me uncomfortable. Perhaps it was because it had remained unchanged for so long. The old horsehair chairs, with their shiny mahogany frames, showed by the slightly worn places in the carpet before them that they had not deviated an inch from their position for many years. The carpets—carpets that reached to the very baseboards and gave under one's feet with yielding of heavy padding beneath—were bright under beds and wardrobes, while in the centers of the rooms they had faded into the softness of old tapestry.

Maggie, I remember, on our arrival moved a chair from the wall in the library, and immediately put it back again, with a glance to see if I had observed her.

"It's nice and clean, Miss Agnes," she said. "A—I kind of feel that a little dirt would make it more homelike."

"I'm sure I don't see why," I replied, rather sharply. "I've lived in a tolerably clean house, most of my life."

Maggie, however, was digging a heel into the padded carpet. She had chosen a sunny place for the experiment, and a small cloud of dust rose like smoke.

"Germs!" she said. "Just what I expected. We'd better bring the vacuum cleaner out from the city, Miss Agnes. Them carpets haven't been lifted for years."

But paid little attention to her. To Maggie any particle of matter not otherwise classified is a germ, and the prospect of finding dust in that immaculate house was sufficiently thrilling to tide over the strangeness of our first few hours in it.

Once a year I rent a house in the country. When my nephew and niece were children, I did it to take them out of the city during school vacations. Later, when they grew up, it was to be near the country club. But now, with the children married and new families coming along, we were more concerned with dairies than with clubs, and I inquired more carefully about the neighborhood cows than about the neighbor-

10

hood golf links. I had really selected the house at Benton Station because there was a most alluring pasture, with a brook running through it, and violets over the banks. It seemed to me that no cow with a conscience could live in those surroundings and give colicky milk.

Then, the house was cheap. Unbelievably cheap. I suspected sewerage at once, but it seemed to be in the best possible order. Indeed, new plumbing had been put in, and extra bathrooms installed. As old Miss Emily Benton lived there alone, with only an old couple to look after her, it looked odd to see three bathrooms, two of them new, on the second floor. Big tubs and showers, although little old Miss Emily could have bathed in a washbowl and have had room to spare.

I faced the agent downstairs in the parlor, after I had gone over the house. Miss Emily Benton had not appeared and I took it she was away.

"Why all those bathrooms?" I demanded. "Does she use them in rotation?"

He shrugged his shoulders.

"She wished to rent the house, Miss Blakiston. The old-fashioned plumbing—"

"But she is giving the house away," I exclaimed. "Those bathrooms have cost much more than she will get out of it. You and I know that the price is absurd."

He smiled at that. "If you wish to pay more, you may, of course. She is a fine woman, Miss Blakiston, but you can never measure a Benton with any yardstick but their own. The truth is that she wants the house off her hands this summer. I don't know why. It's a good house, and she has lived here all her life. But my instructions, I'll tell you frankly, are to rent it, if I have to give it away."

With which absurd sentence we went out the front door, and I saw the pasture, which decided me.

In view of the fact that I had taken the house for my grandnieces and nephews, it was annoying to find, by the end of June, that I should have to live in it by myself. Willie's boy was having his teeth straightened, and must make daily visits to the dentist, and Jack went to California and took Gertrude and the boys with him.

The first curious thing happened then. I wrote to the agent, saying that I would not use the house, but enclosing a check for its rental, as I had signed the lease. To my surprise, I received in reply a note from Miss Emily herself, very carefully written on thin notepaper.

Although it was years since I had seen her, the exquisite neatness of the letter, its careful paragraphing, its margins so accurate as to give the impression that she had drawn a faint margin line with a lead pencil and then erased it—all these were as indicative of Emily Benton as—well, as the letter was not.

As well as I can explain it, the letter was impulsive, almost urgent. Yet the little old lady I remembered was neither of these things.

My dear Miss Blakiston, she wrote. *But I do hope you will use the house. It was because I wanted to be certain that it would be* occupied *this summer that I asked so low a rent for it.*

12

You may call it a whim if you like, but there are reasons why I wish the house to have a summer tenant. It has, for one thing, never been empty since it was built. It was my father's pride, and his father's before him, that the doors were never locked, even at night. Of course I can not ask a tenant to continue this old custom, but I can ask you to reconsider your decision.

Will you forgive me for saying that you are so exactly the person I should like to see in the house that I feel I can not give you up? So strongly do I feel this that I would, if I dared, enclose your check and beg you to use the house rent free.

Faithfully yours, EMILY BENTON

Gracefully worded and carefully written as the letter was, I seemed to feel behind it some stress of feeling, an excitement perhaps, totally out of proportion to its contents. Years before I had met Miss Emily, even then a frail little old lady, her small figure stiffly erect, her eyes cold, her whole bearing one of reserve. The Bentons, for all their open doors, were known in that part of the country as "proud." I can remember, too, how when I was a young girl my mother had regarded the rare invitations to have tea and tiny cakes in the Benton parlor as commands, no less, and had taken the long carriage ride from the city with complacency. And now Miss Emily, last of the family, had begged me to take the house.

In the end, as has been shown, I agreed. The glamor of the past had perhaps something to do with it. But I have come to a time of life when, failing intimate interests of my own, my neighbors' interests

13

are mine by adoption. To be frank, I came because I was curious. Why, aside from a money consideration, was the Benton house to be occupied by an alien household? It was opposed to every tradition of the family as I had heard of it.

I knew something of the family history: the Reverend Thaddeus Benton, rector of Saint Bartholomew, who had forsaken the frame rectory near the church to build himself the substantial home now being offered me; Miss Emily, his daughter, who must now, I computed, be nearly seventy; and a son whom I recalled faintly as hardly bearing out the Benton traditions of solidity and rectitude.

The Reverend Mr. Benton, I recalled, had taken the stand that his house was his own, and having moved his family into it, had thereafter, save on great occasions, received the congregation individually or *en masse*, in his study at the church. A patriarchal old man, benevolent yet austere, who once, according to a story I had heard in my girlhood, had horsewhipped one of his vestrymen for trifling with the affections of a young married woman in the village!

There was a gap of thirty years in my knowledge of the family. I had, indeed, forgotten its very existence, when by the chance of a newspaper advertisement I found myself involved vitally in its affairs, playing providence, indeed, and both fearing and hating my rôle.

Looking back, there are a number of things that appear rather curious. Why, for instance, did Maggie, my old servant, develop such a dislike for the place? It had nothing to do with the house. She had not seen it when she first refused to go. But her reluctance was evident from the beginning.

"I've just got a feeling about it, Miss Agnes," she said. "I can't explain it, any more than I can explain a cold in the head. But it's there."

At first I was inclined to blame Maggie's "feeling" on her knowledge that the house was cheap. She knew it, as she has, I am sure, read all my letters for years. She has a distrust of a bargain. But later I came to believe that there was something more to Maggie's distrust—as though perhaps a wave of uneasiness, spreading from some unknown source, had engulfed her.

Indeed, looking back over the two months I spent in the Benton house, I am inclined to go even further. If thoughts carry, as I am sure they do, then emotions carry. Fear, hope, courage, despair—if the intention of writing a letter to an absent friend can spread itself halfway across the earth, so that as you write the friend writes also, and your letters cross, how much more should big emotions carry? I have had sweep over me such waves of gladness, such gusts of despair, as have shaken me. Yet with no cause for either. They are gone in a moment. Just for an instant, I have caught and made my own another's joy or grief.

The only inexplicable part of this narrative is that Maggie, neither a psychic nor a sensitive type, caught the terror, as I came to call it, before I did. Perhaps it may be explainable by the fact that her mental processes are comparatively simple, her mind an empty slate that shows every mark made on it.

In a way, this is a study in fear.

Maggie's resentment continued through my decision to use the house, through the packing, through the very moving itself. It took the form of a sort of watchful waiting, although at the time we neither of us realized it, and of dislike of the house and its surroundings. It extended itself to the very garden, where she gathered flowers for the table with a ruthlessness that was almost vicious. And, as July went on, and Miss Emily made her occasional visits, as tiny, as delicate as herself, I had a curious conclusion forced on me. Miss Emily returned her antagonism. I was slow to credit it. What secret and even unacknowledged opposition could there be between my downright Maggie and this little old aristocrat with her frail hands and the soft rustle of silk about her?

In Miss Emily, it took the form of—how strange a word to use in connection with her!—of furtive watchfulness. I felt that Maggie's entrance, with nothing more momentous than the tea-tray, set her upright in her chair, put an edge to her soft voice, and absorbed her. She was still attentive to what I said. She agreed or dissented. But back of it all, with her eyes on me, she was watching Maggie.

With Maggie the antagonism took no such subtle form. It showed itself in the second best instead of the best china, and a tendency to weak tea, when Miss Emily took hers very strong. And such was the effect of their mutual watchfulness and suspicion, such perhaps was the influence of the staid old house on me, after a time even that fact, of the strong tea, began to strike me as incongruous. Miss Emily was so consistent, so consistently frail and dainty and so—well, unspotted seems to be the word—and so gentle, yet as time went on I began to feel that she hated

Maggie with a real hatred. And there was the strong tea!

Indeed, it was not quite normal, nor was I. For by that time—the middle of July it was before I figured out as much as I have set down in five minutes—by that time I was not certain about the house. It was difficult to say just what I felt about the house. Willie, who came down over a Sunday early in the summer, possibly voiced it when he came down to his breakfast there.

"How did you sleep?" I asked.

"Not very well." He picked up his coffee cup and smiled over it rather sheepishly. "To tell the truth, I got to thinking about things—the furniture and all that," he said vaguely. "How many people have sat in the chairs and seen themselves in the mirror and died in the bed, and so on."

Maggie, who was bringing in the toast, gave a sort of low moan, which she turned into a cough.

"There have been twenty-three deaths in it in the last forty years, Mr. Willie," she volunteered. "That's according to the gardener. And more than half died in that room of yours."

"Put down that toast before you drop it, Maggie," I said. "You're shaking all over. And go out and shut the door."

"Very well," she said, with a meekness behind which she was both indignant and frightened. "But there is one word I might mention before I go, and that is—cats!"

"Cats!" said Willie, as she slammed the door.

"I think it is only one cat," I observed mildly. "It belongs to Miss Emily, I fancy. It manages to be in a lot of places nearly simultaneously, and Maggie swears it is a dozen.''

Willie is not subtle. He is a practical young man with a growing family, and a tendency the last year or two to flesh. But he ate his breakfast thoughtfully.

"Don't you think it's rather isolated?" he asked finally. "Just you three women here?" I had taken Delia, the cook, along.

"We have a telephone," I said, rather loftily. "Although—" I checked myself, Maggie, I felt sure, was listening in the pantry, and I intended to give her wild fancies no encouragement. To utter a thing is, to Maggie, to give it life. By the mere use of the spoken word it ceases to be supposition and becomes fact.

As a matter of fact, my uneasiness about the house resolved itself into an uneasiness about the telephone. It seems less absurd now than it did then. But I remember what Willie said about it that morning on our way to the church.

"It rings at night, Willie," I said. "And when I go there is no one there."

"So do all telephones," he replied briskly. "It's their greatest weakness."

"Once or twice we have found the thing on the floor in the morning. It couldn't blow over or knock itself down."

"Probably the cat," he said, with the patient air of a man arguing with an unreasonable woman. "Of course," he added—we were passing the churchyard then, dominated by what the village called the Benton "mosolem"—"there's a chance that those dead-and-gone Bentons resent anything as modern as a telephone. It might be interesting to see what they would do to a phonograph."

"I'm going to tell you something, Willie," I said. "I am *afraid* of the telephone."

He was completely incredulous. I felt rather ridiculous, standing there in the sunlight of that summer Sabbath and making my confession. But I did it.

"I am afraid of it," I repeated. "I'm desperately sure you will never understand. Because I don't. I can hardly force myself to go to it. I hate the very back corner of the hall where it stands. I—"

I saw his expression then, and I stopped, furious with myself. Why had I said it? But more important still, why did I feel it? I had not put it into words before, I had not expected to say it then. But the moment I saw it I knew it was true. I had developed an *idée fixe*.

"I have to go downstairs at night and answer it," I added, rather feebly. "It's on my nerves, I think."

"I should think it is," he said, with a note of wonder in his voice. "It doesn't sound like you. A telephone!" But just at the church door he stopped me, a hand on my arm.

"Look here," he said, "don't you suppose it's because you're so dependent on the telephone? You know that if anything goes wrong with it, you're cut off, in a way. And there's another point—you get all your news over it, good and bad." He had difficulty, I think, in finding the words he wanted. "It's—it's vital," he said. "So you attach too much importance to it, and it gets to be an obsession."

"Very likely," I assented. "The whole thing is idiotic, anyhow."

19

But—was it idiotic?

I am endeavoring to set things down as they seemed to me at the time, not in the light of subsequent events. For, if this narrative has any interest at all, it is a psychological one. I have said that it is a study in fear, but perhaps it would be more accurate to say that it is a study of the mental reaction to crime, of its effects on different minds, more or less remotely connected with it.

That my analysis of my impressions in the church that morning are not colored by subsequent events is proved by the fact that under cover of that date, July 16th, I made the following entry:

Why do Maggie and Miss Benton distrust each other?

I realized it even then, although I did not consider it serious, as is evidenced by the fact that I follow it with a recipe for fruit gelatin, copied from the newspaper.

It was a calm and sunny Sunday morning. The church windows were wide open, and a butterfly came in and set the choir boys to giggling. At the end of my pew a stained-glass window to Carlo Benton—the name came like an echo from the forgotten past—sent a shower of colored light over Willie, turned my blue silk to most unspinsterly hues, and threw a sort of summer radiance over Miss Emily herself, in the seat ahead.

She sat quite alone, impeccably neat, even to her profile. She was so orderly, so well balanced, one stitch of her hand-sewed organdy collar was so clearly identical with every other, her very seams, if you can understand it, ran so exactly where they should, that she set me to pulling myself straight. I am rather casual as to seams.

After a time I began to have a curious feeling about her. Her head was toward the rector, standing in a sort of white nimbus of sunlight, but I felt that Miss Emily's entire attention was on our pew, immediately behind her. I find I can not put it into words, unless it was that her back settled into more rigid lines. I glanced along the pew. Willie's face wore a calm and slightly somnolent expression. But Maggie, in her far end—she is very high church and always attends—Maggie's eyes were glued almost fiercely to Miss Emily's back. And just then Miss Emily herself stirred, glanced up at the window and, turning slightly, returned Maggie's glance with one almost as malevolent. I have hesitated over that word. It seems strong now, but at the time it was the one that came into my mind.

When it was over, it was hard to believe that it had happened. And even now, with everything else clear, I do not pretend to explain Maggie's attitude. She knew, in some strange way. But she did not know that she knew—which sounds like nonsense and is as near as I can come to getting it down in words.

Willie left that night, the 16th, and we settled down to quiet days, and, for a time, to undisturbed nights. But on the following Wednesday, by my journal, the telephone commenced to bother me again. Generally speaking, it rang rather early, between eleven o'clock and midnight. But on the following Saturday night I find I have recorded the hour as 2 a.m.

21

In every instance the experience was identical. The telephone never rang the second time. When I went downstairs to answer it—I did not always go—there was the buzzing of the wire, and there was nothing else. It was on the twenty-fourth that I had the telephone inspected and reported in normal condition, and it is possibly significant that for three days afterward my record shows not a single disturbance.

But I do not regard the strange calls over the telephone as so important as my attitude to them. The plain truth is that my fear of the calls extended itself in a few days to cover the instrument, and more than that, to the part of the house it stood in. Maggie never had this, nor did she recognize it in me. Her fear was a perfectly simple although uncomfortable one, centering around the bedrooms where, in each bed, she nightly saw dead and gone Bentons laid out in all the decorum of the best linen.

On more than one evening she came to the library door, with an expression of mentally looking over her shoulder, and some such dialogue would follow:

"D'you mind if I turn the bed down now, Miss Agnes?"

"It's very early."

"S'almost eight." When she is nervous she cuts verbal corners.

"You know perfectly well that I dislike having the beds disturbed until nine o'clock, Maggie."

"I'm going out."

"You said that last night, but you didn't go."

Silence.

"Now, see here, Maggie, I want you to overcome this feeling of"—I hesitated—"of fear. When you have really seen or heard something, it will be time enough to be nervous."

"Humph!" said Maggie on one of these occasions, and edged into the room. It was growing dusk. "It will be too late then, Miss Agnes. And another thing. You're a brave woman. I don't know as I've seen a braver. But I notice you keep away from the telephone after dark."

The general outcome of these conversations was that, to avoid argument, I permitted the preparation of my room for the night at an earlier and yet earlier hour, until at last it was done the moment I was dressed for dinner.

It is clear to me now that two entirely different sorts of fear actuated us. For by that time I had to acknowledge that there was fear in the house. Even Delia, the cook, had absorbed some of Maggie's terror; possibly traceable to some early impressions of death which connected themselves with a four-post bedstead.

Of the two sorts of fear, Delia's and Maggie's symptoms were subjective. Mine, I still feel, were objective.

It was not long before the beginning of August, and during a lull in the telephone matter, that I began to suspect that the house was being visited at night.

There was nothing I could point to with any certainty as having been disturbed at first. It was a matter of a book misplaced on the table, of my sewing-basket open when I always leave it closed, of a burnt match on the floor, whereas it is one of my orderly habits never to leave burnt matches around.

23

And at last the burnt match became a sort of clue, for I suspected that it had been used to light one of the candles that sat in holders of every sort, on the top of the library shelves.

I tried getting up at night and peering over the banisters, but without result. And I was never sure as to articles that they had been moved. I remained in that doubting suspicious halfway ground that is worse than certainty. And there was the matter of motive. I could not get away from that. What possible purpose could an intruder have, for instance, in opening my sewing-basket or moving the dictionary two inches on the center table?

Yet the feeling persisted, and on the second of August I find this entry in my journal:

Right-hand brass, eight inches; left-hand brass, seven inches; carved-wood—Italian—five and three quarter inches each; old glass on mantelpiece—seven inches.

And below this, dated the third:

Last night, between midnight and daylight, the candle in the glass holder on the right side of the mantel was burned down one and one-half inches.

I should, no doubt, have set a watch on my nightly visitor after making this discovery—and one that was apparently connected with it—nothing less than

24

Delia's report that there were candle droppings over the border of the library carpet. But I have admitted that this is a study in fear, and a part of it is my own.

I was afraid. I was afraid of the night visitor, but, more than that, I was afraid of the fear. It had become a real thing by that time, something that lurked in the lower back hall waiting to catch me by the throat, to stop my breath, to paralyze me so I could not escape. I never went beyond that point.

Yet I am not a cowardly woman. I have lived alone too long for that. I have closed too many houses at night and gone upstairs in the dark to be afraid of darkness. And even now I can not, looking back, admit that I was afraid of the darkness there, although I resorted to the weak expedient of leaving a short length of candle to burn itself out in the hall when I went up to bed.

I have seen one of Willie's boys wake up at night screaming with a terror he could not describe. Well, it was much like that with me, except that I was awake and horribly ashamed of myself.

On the fourth of August I find in my journal the single word *flour*. It recalls both my own cowardice at that time, and an experiment I made. The telephone had not bothered us for several nights, and I began to suspect a connection of this sort: when the telephone rang, there was no night visitor, and *vice versa*. I was not certain.

Delia was setting bread that night in the kitchen, and Maggie was reading a ghost story from the evening paper. There was a fine sifting of flour over the table, and it gave me my idea. When I went up to bed that night, I left a powdering of flour here and there on the lower floor, at the door into the library, a patch by the table, and—going back rather uneasily—one near the telephone.

I was up and downstairs before Maggie the next morning. The patches showed trampling. In the doorway they were almost obliterated, as by the trailing of a garment over them, but by the fireplace there were two prints quite distinct. I knew when I saw them that I had expected the marks of Miss Emily's tiny foot, although I had not admitted it before. But these were not Miss Emily's. They were large, flat, substantial, and one showed a curious marking around the edge that— It was my own! The marking was the knitted side of my bedroom slipper. I had, so far as I could tell, gone downstairs, in the night, investigated the candles, possibly in darkness, and gone back to bed again.

The effect of the discovery on me was—well, undermining. In all the uneasiness of the past few weeks I had at least had full confidence in myself. And now that was gone. I began to wonder how much of the things that had troubled me were real, and how many I had made for myself.

To tell the truth, by that time the tension was almost unbearable. My nerves were going, and there was no reason for it. I kept telling myself that. In the mirror I looked white and anxious, and I had a sense of approaching trouble. I caught Maggie watching me, too, and on the seventh I find in my journal the words: *Insanity is often only a formless terror.*

On the Sunday morning following that I found three burnt matches in the library fireplace, and one of the candles in the brass holders was almost gone. I sat most of the day in that room, wondering what would happen to me if I lost my mind. I knew that Maggie was watching me, and I made one of those absurd hypotheses to myself that we all do at times. If any of the family came, I would know that she had sent for them, and that I was really deranged! It had been a long day, with a steady summer rain that had not cooled the earth, but only set it steaming. The air was like hot vapor, and my hair clung to my moist forehead. At about four o'clock Maggie started chasing a fly with a folded newspaper. She followed it about the lower floor from room to room, making little harsh noises in her throat when she missed it. The sound of the soft thud of the paper on walls and furniture seemed suddenly more than I could bear.

"For heaven's sake!" I cried. "Stop that noise, Maggie." I felt as though my eyes were starting from my head.

"It's a fly," she said doggedly, and aimed another blow at it. "If I don't kill it, we'll have a million. There, it's on the mantel now, I never—"

I felt that if she raised the paper club once more I should scream. So I got up quickly and caught her wrist. She was so astonished that she let the paper drop, and there we stood, staring at each other. I can still see the way her mouth hung open.

"Don't!" I said. And my voice sounded thick even to my own ears. "Maggie—I can't stand it!"

"My God, Miss Agnes!"

Her tone brought me up sharply. I released her arm.

"I—I'm just nervous, Maggie," I said, and sat down. I was trembling violently.

I was sane. I knew it then as I know it now. But I was not rational. Perhaps to most of us come now and then times when they realize that some act, or some thought, is not balanced, as though, for a moment or an hour, the control was gone from the brain. Or—and I think this was the feeling I had— that some other control was in charge. Not the Agnes Blakiston I knew, but another Agnes Blakiston, perhaps, was exerting a temporary dominance, a hectic, craven, and hateful control.

That is the only outburst I recall. Possibly Maggie may have others stored away. She has a tenacious memory. Certainly it was my nearest approach to violence. But it had the effect of making me set a watch on myself.

Possibly it was coincidence. Probably, however, Maggie had communicated with Willie. But two days later young Martin Sprague, Freda Sprague's son, stopped his car in the drive and came in. He is a nerve specialist, and very good, although I can remember when he came down in his night drawers to one of his mother's dinner-parties.

"Thought I would just run in and see you," he said. "Mother told me you were here. By George, Miss Agnes, you look younger than ever."

"Who told you to come, Martie?" I asked.

"Told me? I don't have to be told to visit an old friend."

Well, he asked himself to lunch, and looked over the house, and decided to ask Miss Emily if she would sell an old Japanese cabinet inlaid with mother of pearl that I would not have had as a gift. And, in the end, I told him my trouble, of the fear that seemed to

28

center around the telephone, and the sleepwalking.

He listened carefully. "Ever get any bad news over the telephone?" he asked.

One way and another, I said I had had plenty of it. He went over me thoroughly, and was inclined to find my experience with the flour rather amusing than otherwise. "It's rather good, that," he said. "Setting a trap to catch yourself. You'd better have Maggie sleep in your room for a while. Well, it's all pretty plain, Miss Agnes. We bury some things as deep as possible, especially if we don't want to remember that they ever happened. But the mind's a queer thing. It holds on pretty hard, and burying is not destroying. Then we get tired or nervous—maybe just holding the thing down and pretending it is not there makes us nervous—and up it pops, like the ghost of a buried body, and raises hell. You don't mind that, do you?" he added anxiously. "It's exactly what those things do raise."

"*But*," I demanded irritably, "who rings the telephone at night? I dare say you don't contend that I go out at night and call the house, and then come back and answer the call, do you?"

He looked at me with a maddening smile.

"Are you sure it really rings?" he asked.

And so bad was my nervous condition by that time, so undermined was my self-confidence, that I was not certain! And this in face of the fact that it invariably roused Maggie as well as myself.

On the eleventh of August Miss Emily came to tea. The date does not matter, but by following the chronology of my journal I find I can keep my narrative in proper sequence.

I had felt better that day. So far as I could determine, I had not walked in my sleep again, and there was about Maggie an air of cheerfulness and relief which showed that my condition was more nearly normal than it had been for some time. The fear of the telephone and of the back hall was leaving me, too. Perhaps Martin Sprague's matter-of-fact explanation had helped me. But my own theory had always been the one I recorded at the beginning of this narrative—that I caught and—well, registered is a good word—that I registered an overwhelming fear from some unknown source.

I spied Miss Emily as she got out of the hack that day, a cool little figure clad in a thin black silk dress, with the sheerest possible white collars and cuffs. Her small bonnet with its crêpe veil was faced with white, and her carefully crimped gray hair showed a wavy border beneath it. Mr. Staley, the station hackman, handed her the knitting-bag without which she was seldom seen. It was two weeks since she had been there, and she came slowly up the walk, looking from side to side at the perennial borders, then in full August bloom.

She smiled when she saw me in the doorway, and said, with the little anxious pucker between her eyes that was so childish, "Don't you think peonies are better cut down at this time of year?" She took a folded handkerchief from her bag and dabbed at her face, where there was no sign of dust to mar its old freshness. "It gives the lilies a better chance, my dear."

I led her into the house, and she produced a gay bit of knitting, a baby afghan, by the signs. She smiled at me over it.

"I am always one baby behind," she explained and fell to work rapidly. She had lovely hands, and I suspected them of being her one vanity.

Maggie was serving tea with her usual grudging reluctance, and I noticed then that when she was in the room Miss Emily said little or nothing. I thought it probable that she did not approve of conversing before servants, and would have let it go at that had I not, as I held out Miss Emily's cup, caught her looking at Maggie. I had a swift impression of antagonism again, of alertness and something more. When Maggie went out, Miss Emily turned to me.

"She is very capable, I fancy."

"Very. Entirely too capable."

"She looks sharp," said Miss Emily. It was a long time since I had heard the word so used, but it was very apt. Maggie was indeed sharp. But Miss Emily launched into a general dissertation on servants, and Maggie's sharpness was forgotten.

It was, I think, when she was about to go that I asked her about the telephone.

"Telephone?" she inquired. "Why, no. It has always done very well. Of course, after a heavy snow in the winter, sometimes—"

She had a fashion of leaving her sentences unfinished. They trailed off, without any abrupt break.

"It rings at night."

"Rings?"

"I am called frequently, and when I get to the

phone, there is no one there."

Some of my irritation doubtless got into my voice, for Miss Emily suddenly drew away and stared at me.

"But—that is very strange. I—"

She had gone pale. I saw that now. And quite suddenly she dropped her knitting-bag. When I restored it to her, she was very calm and poised, but her color had not come back.

"It has always been very satisfactory," she said. "I don't know that it ever—"

She considered, and began again. "Why not just ignore it? If someone is playing a malicious trick on you, the only thing is to ignore it."

Her hands were shaking, although her voice was quiet. I saw that when she tried to tie the ribbons of the bag. And—I wondered at this, in so gentle a soul—there was a hint of anger in her tones. There was an edge to her voice.

That she could be angry was a surprise. And I found that she could also be obstinate. For we came to an *impasse* over the telephone in the next few minutes, and over something so absurd that I was nonplussed. It was over her unqualified refusal to allow me to install a branch wire to my bedroom.

"But," I expostulated, "when one thinks of the convenience, and—"

"I am sorry." Her voice had a note of finality. "I dare say I am old-fashioned, but—I do not like changes. I shall have to ask you not to interfere with the telephone."

I could hardly credit my senses. Her tone was one of reproof, plus decision. It convicted me of an indiscretion. If I had asked to take the roof off and replace it with silk umbrellas, it might have been justified. But to a request to move the telephone!

"Of course, if you feel that way about it," I said, "I shall not touch it."

I dropped the subject, a trifle ruffled, I confess, and went upstairs to fetch a box in which Miss Emily was to carry away some flowers from the garden.

It was when I was coming down the staircase that I saw Maggie. She had carried the hall candlesticks, newly polished, to their places on the table, and was standing, a hand on each one, staring into the old Washington mirror in front of her. From where she was she must have had a full view of Miss Emily in the library. And Maggie was bristling. It was the only word for it.

She was still there when Miss Emily had gone, blowing on the mirror and polishing it. And I took her to task for her unfriendly attitude to the little old lady.

"You practically threw her muffins at her," I said. "And I must speak again about the cups—"

"What does she come snooping around for, anyhow?" she broke in. "Aren't we paying for her house? Didn't she get down on her bended knees and beg us to take it?"

"Is that any reason why we should be uncivil?"

"What I want to know is this," Maggie said truculently. "What right has she to come back and spy on us? For that's what she's doing, Miss Agnes. Do you know what she was at when I looked in at her? She was running a finger along the baseboard to see if it was clean! And what's more, I caught her at it once before, in the back hall, when she was pretending to telephone for the station hack."

It was that day, I think, that I put fresh candles in all the holders downstairs. I had made a resolution like this—to renew the candles, and to lock myself in my room and threw the key over the transom to Maggie. If, in the mornings that followed, the candles had been used, it would prove that Martin Sprague was wrong, that even footprints could lie, and that someone was investigating the lower floor at night. For while my reason told me that I had been the intruder, my intuition continued to insist that my sleepwalking was a result, not a cause. In a word, I had gone downstairs because I knew that there had been, and might be again, a night visitor.

Yet there was something of comedy in that night's precautions, after all.

At ten-thirty I was undressed, and Maggie had, with rebellion in every line of her, locked me in. I could hear her, afterward, running along the hall to her own room and slamming the door. Then, a moment later, the telephone rang.

It was too early, I reasoned, for the night calls. It might be anything, a telegram at the station, Willie's boy run over by an automobile, Gertrude's children ill. A dozen possibilities ran through my mind.

And Maggie would not let me out!

"You're not going downstairs," she called, from a safe distance.

"Maggie!" I cried sharply. And banged at the door. The telephone was ringing steadily. "Come here at once."

"Miss Agnes," she beseeched, "you go to bed and

don't listen. There'll be nothing there, for all your trouble," she said, in a quavering voice. "It's nothing human that rings that bell."

Finally, however, she freed me, and I went down the stairs. I had carried down a lamp, and my nerves were vibrating to the rhythm of the bell's shrill summons. But, strangely enough, the fear had left me. I find, as always, that it is difficult to put into words. I did not relish the excursion to the lower floor. I resented the jarring sound of the bell. But the terror was gone.

I went back to the telephone. Something that was living and moving was there. I saw its eyes, lower than mine, reflecting the lamp like twin lights. I was frightened, but still it was not the *fear*. The twin lights leaped forward—and proved to be the eyes of Miss Emily's cat, which had been sleeping on the stand!

I answered the telephone. To my surprise it was Miss Emily herself, a quiet and very dignified voice which apologized for disturbing me at that hour, and went on:

"I feel that I was very abrupt this afternoon, Miss Blakiston. My excuse is that I have always feared change. I have lived in a rut too long, I'm afraid. But of course, if you feel you would like to move the telephone, or put in an upstairs instrument, you may do as you like."

She seemed, having got me there, unwilling to ring off. I got a curious effect of reluctance over the telephone, and there was one phrase that she repeated several times.

"I do not want to influence you. I want you to do just what you think best."

The fear was entirely gone by the time she rang off. I felt, instead, a sort of relaxation that was most comforting. The rear hall, a cul-de-sac of nervousness in the daytime and of horror at night, was suddenly transformed by the light of my lamp into a warm and cheerful refuge from the darkness of the lower floor. The purring of the cat, comfortably settled on the telephone stand, was as cheering as the singing of a kettle on a stove. On the rack near me my garden hat and an old Paisley shawl made a grotesque human effigy.

I sat back in the low wicker chair and surveyed the hallway. Why not, I considered, do away now with the fear of it? If I could conquer it like this at midnight, I need never succumb again to it in the light.

The cat leaped to the stand beside me and stood there, waiting. He was an intelligent animal, and I am like a good many spinsters. I am not more fond of cats than other people, but I understand them better. And it seemed to me that he and I were going through some familiar program, of which a part had been neglected. The cat neither sat nor lay, but stood there, waiting.

So at last I fetched the shawl from the rack and made him a bed on the stand. It was what he had been waiting for. I saw that at once. He walked onto it, turned around once, lay down, and closed his eyes.

I took up my vigil. I had been the victim of a fear I

was determined to conquer. The house was quiet. Maggie had retired shriveled to bed. The cat slept on the shawl.

And then—I felt the fear returning. It welled up through my tranquillity like a flood, and swept me with it. I wanted to shriek. I was afraid to shriek. I longed to escape. I dared not move. There had been no sound, no motion. Things were as they had been.

It may have been one minute or five that I sat there. I do not know. I only know that I sat with fixed eyes, not even blinking, for fear of even for a second shutting out the sane and visible world about me. A sense of deadness commenced in my hands and worked up my arms. My chest seemed flattened.

Then the telephone bell rang.

The cat leaped to his feet. Somehow I reached forward and took down the receiver.

"Who is it?" I cried, in a voice that was thin, I knew, and unnatural.

The telephone is not a perfect medium. It loses much that we wish to register but, also, it registers much that we may wish to lose. Therefore when I say that I distinctly heard a gasp, followed by heavy difficult breathing, over the telephone, I must beg for credence. It is true. Someone at the other end of the line was struggling for breath.

Then there was complete silence, I realized, after a moment, that the circuit had been stealthily cut, and that my conviction was verified by Central's demand, a moment later, of what number I wanted. I was, at first, unable to answer her. When I did speak, my voice was shaken.

"What number, please?" she repeated, in a bored tone. There is nothing in all the world so bored as the voice of a small-town telephone operator.

"You called," I said.

"Beg y'pardon. Must have been a mistake," she replied glibly, and cut me off.

Chapter 2

It may be said, and with truth, that so far I have recorded little but subjective terror, possibly easily explained by my occupancy of an isolated house, plus a few unimportant incidents, capable of various interpretations. But the fear was, and is today as I look back, a real thing. As real—and as difficult to describe—as a chill, for instance. A severe mental chill it was, indeed.

I went upstairs finally to a restless night, and rose early, after only an hour or so of sleep. One thing I was determined on—to find out, if possible, the connection between the terror and the telephone. I breakfasted early, and was dressing to go to the village when I had a visitor, no other than Miss Emily herself. She looked fluttered and perturbed at the unceremonious hour of her visit—she was the soul of convention—and explained, between breaths as it were, that she had come to apologize for the day before. She had hardly slept. I must forgive her. She had been very nervous since her brother's death, and

39

small things upset her.

How much of what I say of Miss Emily depends on my later knowledge, I wonder? Did I notice then that she was watching me furtively, or is it only on looking back that I recall it? I do recall it—the hall door open and a vista of smiling garden beyond, and silhouetted against the sunshine. Miss Emily's frail figure and searching, slightly uplifted face. There was something in her eyes that I had not seen before—a sort of exaltation. She was not, that morning, the Miss Emily who ran a finger along her baseboards to see if we dusted them.

She had walked out, and it had exhausted her. She breathed in little gasps.

"I think," she said at last, "that I must telephone for Mr. Staley. I am never very strong in hot weather."

"Please let me call him for you, Miss Emily."

I am not a young woman, and she was at least sixty-five. But, because she was so small and frail, I felt almost a motherly anxiety for her that morning.

"I think I should like to do it, if you don't mind. We are old friends. He always comes promptly when I call him."

She went back alone, and I waited in the doorway. When she came out, she was smiling, and there was more color in her face.

"He is coming at once. He is always very thoughtful for me."

Now, without any warning, something that had been seething since her breathless arrival took shape in my mind, and became—suspicion. What if it had been Miss Emily who had called me the second time

40

to the telephone, and having established the connection, had waited, breathing hard, for—what?

It was fantastic, incredible in the light of that brilliant summer day. I looked at her, dainty and exquisite as ever, her ruchings fresh and white, her very face indicative of decorum and order, her wistful old mouth still rather like a child's, her eyes, always slightly upturned because of her diminutive height, so that she had habitually a look of adoration.

"One of earth's saints," the rector had said to me on Sunday morning. "A good woman, Miss Blakiston, and a sacrifice to an unworthy family."

Suspicion is like the rain. It falls on the just and on the unjust. And that morning I began to suspect Miss Emily. I had no idea of what.

On my mentioning an errand in the village she promptly offered to take me with her in the Staley hack. She had completely altered in manner. The strain was gone. In her soft low voice, as we made our way to the road, she told me the stories of some of the garden flowers.

"The climbing rose over the arch, my dear," she said, "my mother brought from England on her wedding journey. People have taken cuttings from it again and again, but the cuttings never thrive. A bad winter, and they are gone. But this one has lived. Of course now and then it freezes down."

She chattered on, and my suspicions grew more and more shadowy. They would have gone, I think, had not Maggie called me back with a grocery list.

"A sack of flour," she said, "and some green vegetables, and—Miss Agnes, that woman was down on her knees beside the telephone!—and bluing for

41

the laundry, and I guess that's all."

The telephone! It was always the telephone. We drove on down the lane, eyed somnolently by spotted cows and incurious sheep, and all the way Miss Emily talked. She was almost garrulous. She asked the hackman about his family and stopped the vehicle to pick up a peddler, overburdened with his pack. I watched her with amazement. Evidently this was Mr. Staley's Miss Emily. But it was not mine.

But I saw mine, too, that morning. It was when I asked the hackman to put me down at the little telephone building. I thought she put her hand to her throat, although the next moment she was only adjusting the ruching at her neck.

"You—you have decided to have the second telephone put in, then?"

I hesitated. She so obviously did not want it installed. And was I to submit meekly to the fear again, without another effort to vanquish it?

"I think not, dear Miss Emily," I said at last, smiling at her drawn face. "Why should I disturb your lovely old house and its established order?"

"But I want you to do just what you think best," she protested. She had put her hands together. It was almost a supplication.

As to the strange night calls, there was little to be learned. The night operator was in bed. The manager made a note of my complaint, and promised an investigation, which, having had experience with telephone investigations, I felt would lead nowhere. I left the building, with my grocery list in my hand.

The hack was gone, of course. But—I may have imagined it—I thought I saw Miss Emily peering at me from behind the bonnets and hats in the milliner's window.

I did not investigate. The thing was enough on my nerves as it was.

Maggie served me my luncheon in a sort of strained silence. She observed once, as she brought me my tea, that she was giving me notice and intended leaving on the afternoon train. She had, she stated, holding out the sugar-bowl to me at arm's length, stood a great deal in the way of irregular hours from me, seeing as I would read myself to sleep, and let the light burn all night, although very fussy about the bills. But she had reached the end of her tether, and you could grate a lemon on her most anywhere, she was that covered with gooseflesh.

"Goose-flesh about what?" I demanded. "And either throw the sugar to me or come closer."

"I don't know about what," she said sullenly. "I'm just scared."

And for once Maggie and I were in complete harmony. I, too, was "just scared."

We were, however, both of us much nearer a solution of our troubles than we had any idea of. I say solution, although it but substituted one mystery for another. It gave tangibility to the intangible, indeed, but I cannot see that our situation was any better. I, for one, found myself in the position of having a problem to solve, and no formula to solve it with.

The afternoon was quiet. Maggie and the cook were in the throes of jelly-making, and I had picked up a narrative history of the county, written most pedantically, although with here and there a touch of heavy lightness, by Miss Emily's father, the Reverend

Samuel Thaddeus Benton.

On the fly-leaf she had inscribed: *Written by my dear father during the last year of his life, and published after his death by the parish to which he had given so much of his noble life.*

The book left me cold, but the inscription warmed me. Whatever feeling I might have had about Miss Emily died of that inscription. A devoted and self-sacrificing daughter, a woman both loving and beloved, that was the Miss Emily of the dedication to *Fifty years in Bolivar County.*

In the middle of the afternoon Maggie appeared, with a saucer and a teaspoon. In the saucer she had poured a little of the jelly to test it, and she was blowing on it when she entered. I put down my book.

"Well!" I said. "Don't tell me you're not dressed yet. You've just got about time for the afternoon train."

She gave me an imploring glance over the saucer. "You might just take a look at this, Miss Agnes," she said. "It jells around the edges, but in the middle—"

"I'll send your trunk tomorrow," I said, "and you'd better let Delia make the jelly alone. You haven't much time, and she says she makes good jelly."

She raised anguished eyes to mine. "Miss Agnes," she said, "that woman's never made a glass of jelly in her life before. She didn't even know about putting a silver spoon in the tumblers to keep 'em from breaking."

I picked up *Bolivar County* and opened it, but I could see that the hands holding the saucer were shaking.

"I'm not going, Miss Agnes," said Maggie. (I had, of course, known she would not. The surprising thing to me is that she never learns this fact, although she gives me notice quite regularly. She always thinks that she is really going, until the last.) "Of course you can let that woman make the jelly, if you want. It's your fruit and sugar. But I'm not going to desert you in your hour of need."

"What do I need?" I demanded. "Jelly?"

But she was past sarcasm. She placed the saucer on a table and rolled her stained hands in her apron. "That woman," she said, "what was she doing under the telephone stand?"

She almost immediately burst into tears, and it was some time before I caught what she feared. For she was more concrete than I. And she knew now what she was afraid of. It was either a bomb or fire.

"Mark my words, Miss Agnes," she said, "she's going to destroy the place. What made her set out and rent it for almost nothing if she isn't? And I know who rings the telephone at night. It's her."

"What on earth for?" I demanded, hardly less uneasy than Maggie.

"She wakes us up, so we can get out in time. She's a preacher's daughter. More than likely she draws the line at bloodshed. That's one reason. Maybe there's another. What if by pressing a button somewhere and ringing that bell, it sets off a bomb somewhere?"

"It never has," I observed dryly.

But however absurd Maggie's logic might be, she was firm in her major premise. Miss Emily had been on her hands and knees by the telephone stand, and had, on seeing Maggie, observed that she had dropped the money for the hackman out of her glove.

"Which I don't believe. Her gloves were on the stand. If you'll come back, Miss Agnes, I'll show you how she was."

We made rather an absurd procession, Maggie leading with the saucer, I following, and the cat, appearing from nowhere as usual, bringing up the rear. Maggie placed the jelly on the stand, and dropped on her hands and knees, crawling under the stand, a confused huddle of gingham apron, jelly-stains, and suspicion.

"She had her head down like this," she said, in rather a smothered voice. "I'm her, and you're me. And I says: 'If it's rolled off somewhere I'll find it next time I sweep, and give it back to you.' Well, what d'you think of that! Here it is!"

My attention had by this time been caught by the jelly, now unmistakably solidifying in the center. I moved to the kitchen door to tell Delia to take it off the fire. When I returned, Maggie was digging under the telephone battery-box with a hairpin and muttering to herself.

"Darnation!" she said, "it's gone under!"

"If you do get it," I reminded her, "it belongs to Miss Emily."

There is a curious strain of cupidity in Maggie. I have never been able to understand it. With her own money she is as free as air. But let her see a chance for illegitimate gain, of finding a penny on the street, of not paying her fare on the cars, of passing a bad quarter, and she is filled with an unholy joy. And so today. The jelly was forgotten. Terror was gone. All that existed for Maggie was a twenty-five cent piece under a battery box.

Suddenly she wailed: "It's gone, Miss Agnes. It's clean under!"

"Good heavens, Maggie! What difference does it make?"

"W'you mind if I got the ice-pick and unscrewed the box?"

My menage is always notoriously short of tools.

I forbade it at once, and ordered her back to the kitchen, and after a final squint along the carpet, head flat, she dragged herself out and to her feet.

"I'll get the jelly off," she said, "and then maybe a hat pin'll reach it. I can see the edge of it."

A loud crack from the kitchen announced that cook had forgotten the silver spoon, and took Maggie off on a jump. I went back to the library and *Bolivar County* and, I must confess, to a nap in my chair.

I was roused by the feeling that someone was staring at me. My eyes focused first on the ice-pick, then, as I slowly raised them, on Maggie's face, set in hard and uncompromising lines.

"I'd thank you to come with me," she said stiffly.

"Come where?"

"To the telephone."

I groaned inwardly. But, because submission to Maggie's tyranny has become a firm habit with me, I rose. I saw then that she held a dingy quarter in one hand.

Without a word she turned and stalked ahead of me into the hall. It is curious, looking back and remembering that she had then no knowledge of the significance of things, to remember how hard and inexorable her back was. Viewed through the light of what followed, I have never been able to visualize Maggie moving down the hall. It has always been a menacing figure, rather shadowy than real. And the hall itself takes on grotesque proportions, becomes inordinately long, an infinity of hall, fading away into time and distance.

Yet it was only a moment, of course, until I stood by the telephone. Maggie had been at work. The wooden box which covered the battery-jars had been removed, and lay on its side. The battery-jars were uncovered, giving an effect of mystery unveiled, a sort of shamelessness, of destroyed illusion.

Maggie pointed. "There's a paper under one of the jars," she said. "I haven't touched it, but I know well enough what it is."

I have not questioned Maggie on this point, but I am convinced that she expected to find a sort of final summons, of death's visiting-card, for one or the other of us.

The paper was there, a small folded scrap, partially concealed under a jar.

"Them prints was there, too," Maggie said, noncommittally.

The box had accumulated the fluctuant floating particles of months, possibly years—lint from the hall carpet giving it a reddish tinge. And in this light and evanescent deposit, fluttered by a breath, fingers had moved, searched, I am tempted to say groped, although the word seems absurd for anything so small. The imprint of Maggie's coin and of her attempts for salvage were at the edge and quite distinct from the others.

I lifted the jar and picked up the paper. It was folded and refolded until it was not much larger than a thumbnail, a rather stiff paper crossed with faint blue lines. I am not sure that I would have opened it— it had been so plainly in hiding, and was obviously not my affair—had not Maggie suddenly gasped and implored me not to look at it. I immediately determined to examine it.

Yet, after I had read it twice, it had hardly made an impression on my mind. There are some things so incredible that the brain automatically rejects them. I looked at the paper. I read it with my eyes. But I did not grasp it.

It was not notepaper. It was apparently torn from a tablet of glazed and ruled paper—just such paper, for instance, as Maggie soaks in brandy and places on top of her jelly before tying it up. It had been raggedly torn. The scrap was the full width of the sheet, but only three inches or so deep. It was undated, and this is what it said:

> *To whom it may concern: On the 30th day of May, 1911, I killed a woman (here) in this house. I hope you will not find this until I am dead.*
> (Signed) EMILY BENTON

Maggie had read the confession over my shoulder, and I felt her body grow rigid. As for myself, my first sensation was one of acute discomfort—that we should have exposed the confession to the light of day. Neither of us, I am sure, had really grasped it. Maggie put a trembling hand on my arm.

"The brass of her," she said, in a thin, terrified voice. "And sitting in church like the rest of us. Oh, my God, Miss Agnes, put it back!"

I whirled on her, in a fury that was only an outlet for my own shock.

"Once for all, Maggie," I said, "I'll ask you to wait until you are spoken to. And if I hear that you have so much as mentioned this—piece of paper, out you go and never come back."

But she was beyond apprehension. She was literal, too. She saw, not Miss Emily unbelievably associated with a crime, but the crime itself.

"Who d'you suppose it was, Miss Agnes?"

"I don't believe it at all. Someone has placed it there to hurt Miss Emily."

"It's her writing," said Maggie doggedly.

After a time I got rid of her, and sat down to think in the library. Rather I sat down to reason with myself.

For every atom of my brain was clamoring that this thing was true, that my little Miss Emily, exquisite and fine as she was, had done the thing she claimed to have done. It was her own writing, thin, faintly shaded, as neat and as erect as herself. But even that I would not accept, until I had compared it with such bits of hers as I possessed, the note begging me to take the house, the inscription on the fly-leaf of *Fifty Years in Bolivar County*.

And here was something I could not quite understand. The writing was all of the same order, but while the confession and the inscription in the book were similar, letter for letter, in the note to me there were differences, a change in the "t" in Benton, a fuller and blacker stroke, a variation in the terminals of the letters—it is hard to particularize.

I spent the remainder of the day in the library, going out for dinner, of course, but returning to my refuge again immediately after. Only in the library am I safe from Maggie. By virtue of her responsibility for my wardrobe, she virtually shares my bedroom, but her respect for books she never reads makes her regard a library as at least semi-holy ground. She dusts books with more caution than china, and her respect for a family Bible is greater than her respect for me.

I spent the evening there, Miss Emily's cat on the divan, and the mysterious confession lying before me under the lamp. At night the variation between it and her note to me concerning the house seemed more pronounced. The note looked more like a clumsy imitation of Miss Emily's own hand. Or—perhaps this is nearer—as if, after writing in a certain way for sixty years, she had tried to change her style.

All my logic ended in one conclusion. She must have known the confession was there. Therefore the chances were that she had placed it there. But it was not so simple as that.

Both crime and confession indicated a degree of impulse that Miss Emily did not possess. I have entirely failed with my picture of Miss Emily if the word violence can be associated with her in any way. Miss Emily was a temple, clean-swept, cold, and empty. She never acted on impulse. Every action, almost every word, seemed the result of thought and deliberation.

Yet, if I could believe my eyes, five years before she

had killed a woman in this very house. Possibly in the very room in which I was then sitting.

I find, on looking back, that the terror must have left me that day. It had, for so many weeks, been so much a part of my daily life that I would have missed it had it not been for this new and engrossing interest. I remember that the long French windows of the library reflected the room—like mirrors against the darkness outside, and that once I thought I saw a shadowy movement in one of them, as though a figure moved behind me. But when I turned sharply there was no one there, and Maggie proved to be, as usual after nine o'clock, shut away upstairs.

I was not terrified. And indeed the fear never returned. In all the course of my investigations, I was never again a victim of the unreasoning fright of those earlier days.

My difficulty was that I was asked to believe the unbelievable. It was impossible to reconstruct in that quiet house a scene of violence. It was equally impossible, in view, for instance, of that calm and filial inscription in the history of Bolivar County, to connect Miss Emily with it. She had killed a woman, forsooth! Miss Emily, of the baby afghans, of the weary peddler, of that quiet seat in the church.

Yet I knew now that Miss Emily knew of the confession; knew, at least, of something concealed in that corner of the rear hall which housed the telephone. Had she by chance an enemy who would have done this thing? But to suspect Miss Emily of an enemy was as absurd as to suspect her of a crime.

I was completely at a loss when I put out the light and prepared to close the house. As I glanced back along the hall, I could not help wondering if the telephone, having given up its secret, would continue its nocturnal alarms. As I stood there, I heard the low growl of thunder and the patter of rain against the windows. Partly out of loneliness, partly out of bravado, I went back to the telephone and tried to call Willie. But the line was out of order.

I slept badly. Shortly after I returned I heard a door slamming repeatedly, which I knew meant an open window somewhere. I got up and went into the hall. There was a cold air coming from somewhere below. But as I stood there it ceased. The door above stopped slamming, and silence reigned again.

Maggie roused me early. The morning sunlight was just creeping into the room, and the air was still cool with the night and fresh-washed by the storm.

"Miss Agnes," she demanded, standing over me, "did you let the cat out last night?"

"I brought him in before I went to bed."

"Humph!" said Maggie. "And did I or did I not wash the doorstep yesterday?"

"You ought to know. You said you did."

"Miss Agnes," Maggie said, "that woman was in this house last night. You can see her footprints as plain as day on the doorstep. And what's more, she stole the cat and let out your mother's Paisley shawl."

Which statements, corrected, proved to be true. My old Paisley shawl was gone from the hall-rack, and unquestionably the cat had been on the back doorstep that morning along with the milk bottles. Moreover, one of my fresh candles had been lighted, but had burned for only a moment or two.

That day I had a second visit from young Martin

Sprague. The telephone was in working order again, having unaccountably recovered, and I was using it when he came. He watched me quizzically from a position by the newel-post, as I rang off.

"I was calling Miss Emily Benton," I explained, "but she is ill."

"Still troubled with telephobia?"

"I have other things to worry me, Martin," I said gravely, and let him into the library.

There I made a clean breast of everything. I omitted nothing. The fear, the strange ringing of the telephone bell; the gasping breathing over it the night before; Miss Emily's visit to it. And at last, the discovery.

He took the paper when I offered it to him, and examined it carefully by a window. Then he stood looking out and whistling reflectively. At last he turned back to the room.

"It's an unusual story," he said. "But if you'll give me a little time I'll explain it to you. In the first place, let go of the material things for a moment, and let's deal with minds and emotions. You're a sensitive person, Miss Agnes. You catch a lot of impressions that pass most people by. And, first of all, you've been catching fright from two sources."

"Two sources?"

"Two. Maggie is one. She hates the country. She is afraid of old houses. And she sees in this house only the ghosts of people who have died here."

"I pay no attention to Maggie's fears."

"You only think that. But to go further—you have been receiving waves of apprehension from another source—from the little lady, Miss Emily."

54

"Then you think—"

"Hold on," he said smiling. "I think she wrote that confession. Yes. As a matter of fact, I'm quite sure she did. And she has established a system of espionage on you by means of the telephone. If you had discovered the confession, she knew that there would be a change in your voice, in your manner. If you answered very quickly, as though you had been near the instrument, perhaps in the very act of discovering the paper—don't you get it? And can't you see how her terror affected you even over the wire? Don't you think that, if thought can travel untold distances, fear can? Of course."

"But, Martin!" I exclaimed. "Little Miss Emily a murderess."

He threw up his hands.

"Certainly not," he said. "You're a shrewd woman, Miss Agnes. Do you know that a certain type of woman frequently confesses to a crime she never committed, or had any chance of committing? Look at the police records—confessions of women as to crimes they could only have heard of through the newspapers! I would like to wager that if we had the newspapers of that date that came into this house, we would find a particularly atrocious and mysterious murder being featured—the murder of a woman."

"*You* do not know her," I maintained doggedly. And drew, as best I could, a sketch of Miss Emily, while he listened attentively.

"A pure neurasthenic type," was his comment. "Older than usual, but that is accountable by the sheltered life she has led. The little Miss Emily is still at heart a girl. And a hysterical girl."

55

"She has had enough trouble to develop her."

"Trouble! Has she ever had a genuine emotion? Look at this house. She nursed an old father in it, a bedridden mother, a paretic brother, when she should have been having children. Don't you see it, Miss Agnes? All her emotions have had to be mental. Failing them outside, she provided them for herself. "This"—he tapped the paper in his hand—"this is one."

I had heard of people confessing to crimes they had never committed, and at the time Martin Sprague at least partly convinced me. He was so sure of himself. And when, that afternoon, he telephoned me from the city to say that he was mailing out some old newspapers, I knew quite well what he had found.

"I've thought of something else, Miss Agnes," he said. "If you'll look it up you will probably find that the little lady had had either a shock sometime before that, or a long pull of nursing. Something, anyhow, to set her nervous system to going in the wrong direction."

Late that afternoon, as it happened, I was enabled to learn something of this from a visiting neighbor, and once again I was forced to acknowledge that he might be right.

The neighbors had not been overcordial. I had gathered, from the first, the impression that the members of the Reverend Samuel Thaddeus Benton's congregation did not fancy an interloper among the sacred relics of the historian of Bolivar County. And I had a corroboration of that impression from my visitor of that afternoon, a Mrs. Graves.

"I've been slow in coming, Miss Blakiston," she said, seating herself primly. "I don't suppose you can understand, but this has always been the Benton place, and it seems strange to us to see new faces here."

I replied, with some asperity, that I had not been anxious to take the house, but that Miss Emily had been so insistent that I had finally done so.

It seemed to me that she flashed a quick glance at me.

"She is quite the most loved person in the valley," she said. "And she loves the place. It is— I cannot imagine why she rented the house. She is far from comfortable where she is."

After a time I gathered that she suspected financial stringency as the cause, and I tried to set her mind at rest.

"It cannot be money," I said. "The rent is absurdly low. The agent wished her to ask more, but she refused."

She sat silent for a time, pulling at the fingers of her white silk gloves. And when she spoke again it was of the garden. But before she left she returned to Miss Emily.

"She has had a hard life, in a way," she said. "It is only five years since she buried her brother, and her father not long before that. She has broken a great deal since then. Not that the brother—"

"I understand he was a great care."

Mrs. Graves looked about the room, its shelves piled high with the ecclesiastical library of the late clergyman.

"It was not only that," she said. "When he was—all right, he was an atheist. Imagine, in this house! He had the most terrible books, Miss Blakiston. And, of course, when a man believes there is no hereafter, he is apt to lead a wicked life. There is nothing to hold him back."

Her mind was on Miss Emily and her problems. She moved abstractedly toward the door.

"In this very hall," she said, "I helped Miss Emily to pack all his books into a box, and we sent for Mr. Staley—the hackman at the station, you know—and he dumped the whole thing into the river. We went away with him, and how she cheered up when it was done!"

Martin Sprague's newspapers arrived the next morning. They bore a date of two days before the date of the confession, and contained, rather triumphantly outlined in blue pencil, full details of the murder of a young woman by some unknown assassin. It had been a grisly crime, and the paper was filled with details of a most sensational sort.

Had I been asked, I would have said that Miss Emily's clear, slightly upturned eyes had never glanced beyond the merest headlines of such journalistic reports. But in a letter Martin Sprague set forth a precisely opposite view.

You will probably find, he wrote, *that the little lady is pretty well fed up on such stuff. The calmer and more placid the daily life, the more apt is the secret inner one, in such a circumscribed existence, to be a thriller! You might look over the books in the house. There is a*

58

historic case where a young girl swore she had tossed her little brother to a den of lions (although there were no lions near, and little brother was subsequently found (asleep *in the attic*) *after reading Fox's* Book of Martyrs. *Probably the old gentleman has this joke book in his library.*

I put down his letter and glanced around the room. Was he right, after all? Did women, rational, truthful, devout women, ever act in this strange manner? And if it was true, was it not in its own way as mysterious as everything else?

I was, for a time that day, strongly influenced by Martin Sprague's conviction. It was, for one thing, easier to believe than that Emily Benton had committed a crime. And, as if to lend color to his assertion, the sunlight, falling on the dreary bookshelves, picked out and illuminated dull gilt letters on the brown back of a volume. It was Fox's *Book of Martyrs!*

If I may analyze my sensations at that time, they divided themselves into three parts. The first was fear. That seems to have given away to curiosity, and that, at a later period, to an intense anxiety. Of the three, I have no excuse for the second, save the one I gave myself at the time—that Miss Emily could not possibly have done the thing she claimed to have done, and that I must prove her innocence to myself.

With regard to Martin Sprague's theory, I was divided. I wanted him to be right. I wanted him to be wrong. No picture I could visualize of little old Miss Emily conceivably fitted the type he had drawn. On the other hand, nothing about her could possibly confirm the confession as an actual one.

The scrap of paper became, for the time, my universe. Did I close my eyes, I saw it side by side with the inscription in *Fifty Years in Bolivar County*, and letter for letter, in the same hand. Did the sun shine, I had it in the light, examining it, reading it. To such a point did it obsess me that I refused to allow Maggie to use a tablet of glazed paper she had found in the kitchen table drawer to tie up the jelly-glasses. It seemed, somehow, horrible to me.

At that time I had no thought of going back five years and trying to trace the accuracy or falsehood of the confession. I should not have known how to go about it. Had such a crime been committed, how to discover it at this late day? Whom, in all her sheltered life, could Miss Emily have murdered? In her small world, who could have fallen out and left no sign?

It was impossible, and I knew it. And yet—

Miss Emily was ill. The news came through the grocery boy, who came out every day on a bicycle, and teased the cat and carried away all the pears as fast as they ripened. Maggie brought me the information at luncheon.

"*She's* sick," she said.

There was only one person in both our minds those days.

"Do you mean really ill, or only—"

"The boy says she's breaking up. If you ask me, she caught cold the night she broke in here and took your Paisley shawl. And if you ask my advice, Miss Agnes, you'll get it back again before the heirs step in and claim it. They don't make them shawls nowadays, and she's as like as not to will it to somebody if you don't go after it."

"Maggie," I said quietly, "how do you *know* she has that shawl?"

"How did I know that paper was in the telephone-box?" she countered.

And indeed, by that time Maggie had convinced herself that she had known all along there was something in the telephone battery-box.

"I've a sort of second sight, Miss Agnes," she added. And, with a shrewdness I found later was partially correct: "She was snooping around to see if you'd found the paper, and it came on to rain; so she took the shawl. I should say," said Maggie, lowering her voice, "that as like as not she's been in this house every night since we came."

Late that afternoon I cut some of the roses from the arch for Miss Emily and, wrapping them against the sun, carried them to the village. At the last I hesitated. It was so much like prying. I turned aside at the church intending to leave them there for the altar. But I could find no one in the parish house, and no vessel to hold them.

It was late afternoon. I opened a door and stepped into the old church. I knelt for a moment, and then sat back and surveyed the quiet building. It occurred to me that here one could obtain a real conception of the Benton family, and of Miss Emily. The church had been the realest thing in their lives. It had dominated them, obsessed them. When the Reverend Samuel Thaddeus died, they had built him, not a momument, but a parish house. When Carlo Benton died (however did such an ungodly name come to belong to a Benton?) Miss Emily, according to the story, had done without fresh mourning and built him a window.

I looked at the window. It was extremely ugly, and very devout. And under it was the dead man's name and two dates, 1860 and 1911.

So Carlo Benton had died the year Miss Emily claimed to have done a murder! Another proof, I reflected that Martin Sprague would say. He had been on her hands for a long time, both well and ill. Small wonder if little Miss Emily had fallen to imagining things, or to confessing them.

I looked at the memorial window once more, and I could almost visualize her gathering up the dead man's hateful books, and getting them as quickly as possible out of the house. Quite possibly there were unmentionable volumes among them—de Maupassant, perhaps Boccaccio. I had a distinct picture, too, of Mrs. Graves, lips primly set, assisting her with hands that fairly itched with the righteousness of her actions.

I still held the roses, and as I left the church I decided to lay them on some grave in the churchyard. I thought it quite likely that roses from the same arch had been frequently used for that purpose. Some very young grave, I said to myself, and found one soon enough, a bit of a rectangle of fresh earth, and a jarful of pansies on it. It lay in the shadow of the Benton mausoleum.

That was how I found that Carlo Benton had died on the 27th of May, 1911.

I cannot claim that the fact at the time had any significance for me, or that I saw it in anything more than another verification of Martin Sprague's solution. But it enabled me to reconstruct the Benton household at the date that had grown so significant. The 30th would have probably been the day after the funeral. Perhaps the nurse was still there. He had had a nurse for months, according to Mrs. Graves. And there would have been the airing that follows long illness and death, the opened windows, the packing up or giving away of clothing, the pauses and silences, the sense of strangeness and quiet, the lowered voices. And there would have been, too, that remorseless packing for destruction of the dead atheist's books.

And some time, during that day or the night that followed, little Miss Emily claimed to have committed her crime.

I went home thoughtfully. At the gate I turned and looked back. The Benton Mausoleum was warm in the sunset, and the rose sprays lay, like outstretched arms, across the tiny grave.

Maggie is amazingly efficient. I am efficient myself, I trust, but I modify it with intelligence. It is not to me a vital matter, for instance, if three dozen glasses of jelly sit on a kitchen table a day or two after they are prepared for retirement to the fruit cellar. I rather like to see them, marshaled in their neat rows, capped with sealing wax and paper, and armed with labels. But Maggie has neither sentiment nor imagination. Jelly to her is an institution, not an inspiration. It is subject to certain rules and rites, of which not the least is the formal interment in the fruit-closet.

Therefore, after much protesting that night, I agreed to visit the fruit cellar, and select a spot for the temporary entombing of thirty-six jelly tumblers, which would have been thirty-seven had Delia known the efficacy of a silver spoon. I can recall vividly the mental shift from the confession to that domestic excursion, my own impatience, Maggie's grim determination, and the curious dénouement of that visit.

Chapter 3

I had the very slightest acquaintance with the basement of the Benton house. I knew it was dry and orderly, and with that my interest in it ceased. It was not cemented, but its hard clay floor was almost as solid as macadam. In one end was built a high potato-bin. In another corner two or three old pews from church, evidently long discarded and showing weather-stains, as though they had once served as garden benches, were up ended against the white-washed wall. The fruit-closet, built in of lumber, occupied one entire end, and was virtually a room, with a door and no windows.

Maggie had, she said, found it locked and had had an itinerant locksmith fit a key to it.

"It's all scrubbed and ready," she said. "I found that preserved melon-rind you had for lunch in a corner. 'Twouldn't of kept much longer, so I took it up and opened it. She's probably got all sorts of stuff spoiling in the locked part. Some folks're like that."

Most of the shelves were open, but now, holding

the lamp high, I saw that a closet with a door occupied one end. The door was padlocked. At the time I was interested, but I was, as I remember, much more occupied with Maggie's sense of *meum* and *tuum*, which I considered deficient, and of a small lecture on other people's melon-rinds, which I delivered as she sullenly put away the jelly.

But that night, after I had gone to bed, the memory of that padlock became strangely insistent. There was nothing psychic about the feeling I had. It was perfectly obvious and simple. The house held, or had held, a secret. Yet it was, above stairs, as open as the day. There was no corner into which I might not peer, except— Why was that portion of the fruit-closet locked?

At two o'clock, finding myself unable to sleep, I got up and put on my dressing-gown and slippers. I had refused to repeat the experiment of being locked in. Then, with a candle and a box of matches, I went downstairs. I had, as I have said, no longer any terror of the lower floor. The cat lay as usual on the table in the back hall. I saw his eyes watching me with their curious unblinking stare, as intelligent as two brass buttons. He rose as my light approached, and I made a bed for him of a cushion from a chair, failing my Paisley shawl.

It was after that that I had the curious sense of being led. It was as though I knew that something awaited my discovery, and that my sole volition was whether I should make that discovery or not. It was there, waiting.

I have no explanation for this. And it is quite possible that I might have had it, to find at the end nothing more significant than root beer, for instance, or bulbs for the winter garden.

And indeed, at first sight, what awaited me in the locked closet amounted to anticlimax. For when I had broken the rusty padlock open with a hatchet, and had opened doors with nervous fingers, nothing more startling appeared than a number of books. The shelves were piled high with them, a motley crew of all colors, but dark shades predominating.

I went back to bed, sheepishly enough, and wrapped my chilled feet in an extra blanket. Maggie came to the door about the time I was dozing off and said she had heard hammering downstairs in the cellar some time ago, but she had refused to waken me until the burglars had gone.

"If it *was* burglars," she added, "you're that up-and-ready, Miss Agnes, that I knew if I waked you you'd be downstairs after them. What's a bit of silver to a human life?"

I got her away at last, and she went, muttering something about digging up the cellar floor and finding an uneasy spirit. Then I fell asleep.

I had taken cold that night, and the following morning I spent in bed. At noon Maggie came upstairs, holding at arm's length a book. She kept her face averted, and gave me a slanting and outraged glance.

"This is a nice place we've come to," she said, acidly. "Murder in the telephone and anti-Christ in the fruit cellar!"

"Why, Maggie," I expostulated.

"If these books stay, I go, and that's flat, Miss Agnes," was her *ipse dixit*. She dropped the book on

67

the bed and stalked out, pausing at the door only to throw back, "If this is a clergyman's house, I guess I'd be better out of the church."

I took up the book. It was well-worn, and in the front, in a heavy masculine hand, the owner had written his name—written it large, a bit defiantly, perhaps. It had taken both courage and conviction to bring such a book into that devout household.

I am not quick, mentally, especially when it comes to logical thought. I dare say I am intuitive rather than logical. It was not by any process of reasoning at all, I fancy, that it suddenly seemed strange that there should be books locked away in the cellar. Yet it was strange. For that had been a bookish household. Books were its stock in trade, one may say. Such as I had borrowed from the library had been carefully tended. Torn leaves were neatly repaired. The reference books were alphabetically arranged. And, looking back on my visit to the cellar, I recalled now as inconsistent the disorder of those basement shelves.

I did not reach the truth until, that afternoon, I made a second visit to the cellar. Mrs. Graves had been mistaken. If not all Carlo Benton's proscribed books were hidden there, at least a large portion of his library was piled, in something like confusion, on the shelves. Yet she maintained that they had searched the house, and she herself had been present when the books were packed and taken away to the river.

That afternoon I returned Mrs. Graves's visit. She was at home, and in a sort of flurried neatness that convinced me she had seen me from far up the road.

That conviction was increased by the amazing promptness with which a tea-tray followed my entrance. I had given her tea the day she came to see me, and she was not to be outdone. Indeed, I somehow gained the impression that tray and teapot, and even little cakes, had been waiting, day by day, for my anticipated visit.

It was not hard to set her talking of Carlo Benton and his wickedness. She rose to the bait like a hungry fish. Yet I gathered that, beyond his religious views or lack of them, she knew nothing. But on the matter of the books she was firm. "After the box was ready," she said, "we went to every room and searched it. Miss Emily was set on clearing out every trace. At the last minute I found one called *The Fallacy of Christianity* slipped down behind the dresser in his room, and we put that in."

It was *The Fallacy of Christianity* that Maggie had brought me that morning.

"It is a most interesting story," I observed. "What delicious tea, Mrs. Graves! And then you fastened up the box and saw it thrown into the river. It was quite a ceremony."

"My dear," Mrs. Graves said solemnly, "it was not a ceremony. It was a rite—a significant rite."

How can I reconcile the thoughts I had that afternoon with my later visit to Miss Emily? The little upper room in the village, dominated and almost filled by an old-fashioned bed, and Miss Emily, frail and delicate and beautifully neat, propped with pillows and holding a fine handkerchief, as fresh as the flutings of her small cap, in her hand. On a small stand beside the bed were her Bible, her spectacles, and her quaint old-fashioned gold watch.

And Miss Emily herself? She was altered, shockingly altered. A certain tenseness had gone, a tenseness that had seemed to uphold her frail body and carry her about. Only her eyes seemed greatly alive, and before I left they, too, had ceased their searching of mine and looked weary and old.

And, at the end of my short visit, I had reluctantly reached this conclusion: either Miss Emily had done the thing she confessed to doing, incredible as it might appear, or she thought she had done it; and the thing was killing her.

She knew I had found the confession. I knew that. It was written large over her. What she had expected me to do God only knows. To stand up and denounce her? To summon the law? I do not know.

She said an extraordinary thing, when at last I rose to go. I believe now that it was to give me my chance to speak. Probably she found the suspense intolerable. But I could not do it. I was too surprised, too perplexed, too—well, afraid of hurting her. I had the feeling, I know, that I must protect her. And that feeling never left me until the end.

"I think you must know, my dear," she said, from her pillows, "that I have your Paisley shawl."

I was breathless. "I thought that, perhaps"—I stumbled.

"It was raining that night," she said in her soft, delicate voice. "I have had it dried and pressed. It is not hurt. I thought you would not mind," she concluded.

"It does not matter at all—not in the least," I said unhappily.

I am quite sure now that she meant me to speak then. I can recall the way she fixed her eyes on me, serene and expectant. She was waiting. But to save my life I could not. And she did not. Had she gone as far as she had the strength to go? Or was this again one of those curious pacts of hers—if I spoke or was silent, it was to be?

I do not know.

I do know that we were both silent and that at last, with a quick breath, she reached out and thumped on the floor with a cane that stood beside the bed until a girl came running up from below stairs.

"Get the shawl, Fanny, dear," said Miss Emily, "and wrap it up for Miss Blakiston."

I wanted desperately, while the girl left the room to obey, to say something helpful, something reassuring. But I could not. My voice failed me. And Miss Emily did not give me another opportunity. She thanked me rather formally for the flowers I had brought from her garden, and let me go at last with the parcel under my arm, without further reference to it. The situation was incredible.

Somehow I had the feeling that Miss Emily would never reopen the subject again. She had given me my chance, at who knows what cost, and I had not taken it. There had been something in her good-by—I can not find words for it, but it was perhaps a finality, an effect of a closed door—that I felt without being able to analyze.

I walked back to the house, refusing the offices of Mr. Staley, who met me on the road. I needed to think. But thinking took me nowhere. Only one conclusion stood out as a result of a mile and a half of mental struggle. Something must be done. Miss Emily ought to be helped. She was under a strain that was killing her.

But to help I should know the facts. Only, were there any facts to know? Suppose—just by way of argument, for I did not believe it—that the confession was true; how could I find out anything about it? Five years was a long time. I could not go to the neighbors. They were none too friendly as it was. Besides, the secret, if there was one, was not mine, but was Miss Emily's.

I reached home at last, and smuggled the shawl into the house. I had no intention of explaining its return to Maggie. Yet, small as it was in its way, it offered a problem at once. For Maggie has a penetrating eye and an inquiring nature. I finally decided to take the bull by the horns and hang it in its accustomed place in the hall, where Maggie, finding it at nine o'clock that evening, set up such a series of shrieks and exclamations as surpassed even her own record.

I knitted that evening. It has been my custom for years to knot bedroom slippers for an old ladies' home in which I am interested. Because I can work at them with my eyes shut, through long practice, I find the work soothing. So that evening I knitted at Eliza Klinordlinger's fifth annual right slipper, and tried to develop a course of action.

I began with a major premise—to regard the confession as a real one, until it was proved otherwise. Granted, then, that my little old Miss Emily had killed a woman.

1st—Who was the woman?

2nd—Where is the body?

3rd—What was the reason for the crime?

Question two I had a tentative answer for. However horrible and incredible it seemed, it was at least possible that Miss Emily had substituted the body for the books, and that what Mrs. Graves described as a rite had indeed been one. But that brought up a picture I could not face.

And yet—

I called up the local physician, a Doctor Lingard, that night and asked him about Miss Emily's condition. He was quite frank with me. "It's just a breaking up," he said. "It has come early, because she has had a trying life, and more responsibility than she should have had."

"I have been wondering if a change of scene would not be a good thing," I suggested. But he was almost scornful.

"Change!" he said. "I've been after her to get away for years. She won't leave. I don't believe she has been twelve miles away in thirty years."

"I suppose her brother was a great care," I observed.

It seemed to me that the doctor's hearty voice was a trifle less frank when he replied. But when I rang off I told myself that I, too, was becoming neurasthenic and suspicious. I had, however, learned what I had wanted to know. Miss Emily had had no life outside Bolivar County. The place to look for her story was here, in the immediate vicinity.

That night I made a second visit to the basement. It seemed to me, with those chaotic shelves before me, that something of the haste and terror of a night five

73

years before came back to me, a night when, confronted by the necessity for concealing a crime, the box upstairs had been hurriedly unpacked, its contents hidden here and locked away, and some other content, inert and heavy, had taken the place of the books.

Miss Emily in her high bed, her Bible and spectacles on the stand beside her, her starched pillows, her soft and highbred voice? Or another Miss Emily, panting and terror-stricken, carrying down her armfuls of forbidden books, her slight figure bent under their weight, her ears open for sounds from the silent house? Or that third Miss Emily, Martin Sprague's, a strange wild creature, neither sane nor insane, building a crime out of the fabric of a nightmare? Which was the real Emily Benton?

Or was there another contingency that I had not thought of? Had some secret enemy of Miss Emily's, some hysterical girl from the parish, suffering under a fancied slight, or some dismissed and revengeful servant, taken this strange method of retaliation, done it and then warned the little old lady that her house contained such a paper? I confess that this last thought took hold of me. It offered a way out that I clutched at.

I had an almost frantic feeling by that time that I must know the truth. Suspense was weighing on me. And Maggie, never slow to voice an unpleasant truth, said that night, as she brought the carafe of ice-water to the library, "You're going off the last few days, Miss Agnes." And when I made no reply: "You're sagging around the chin. There's nothing shows age

74

like the chin. If you'd rub a little lemon juice on at night you'd tighten up some."

I ignored her elaborately, but I knew she was right. Heat and sleepless nights and those early days of fear had told on me. And although I ususally disregard Maggie's cosmetic suggestions, culled from the beauty columns of the evening paper, a look in the mirror decided me. I went downstairs for the lemon. At least, I thought it was for the lemon. I am not sure. I have come to be uncertain of my motives. It is distinctly possible that, subconsciously, I was making for the cellar all the time. I only know that I landed there, with a lemon in my hand, at something after eleven o'clock.

The books were piled in disorder on the shelves. Their five years of burial had not hurt them beyond a slight dampness of the leaves. No hand, I believe, had touched them since they were taken from the box where Mrs. Graves had helped to pack them. Then, if I were shrewd, I should perhaps gather something from their very disorder. But, as a matter of fact, I did not.

I would, quite certainly, have gone away as I came, clueless, had I not attempted to straighten a pile of books, dangerously sagging—like my chin!—and threatening a fall. My effort was rewarded by a veritable Niagara of books. They poured over the edge, a few first, then more, until I stood, it seemed, knee-deep in a raging sea of atheism.

Somewhat grimly I set to work to repair the damage, and one by one I picked them up and restored them. I put them in methodically this time, glancing at each title to place the volume upright.

Suddenly, out of the darkness of unbelief, a title caught my eye and held it, *The Handwriting of God*. I knew the book. It had fallen into bad company, but its theology was unimpeachable. It did not belong. It—

I opened it. The Reverend Samuel Thaddeus had written his own name in it, in the cramped hand I had grown to know. Evidently its presence there was accidental. I turned it over in my hands, and saw that it was closed down on something, on several things, indeed. They proved to be a small black notebook, a pair of spectacles, a woman's handkerchief.

I stood there looking at them. They might mean nothing but the accidental closing of a book, which was mistakenly placed in bad company, perhaps by Mrs. Graves. I was inclined to doubt her knowledge of religious literature. Or they might mean something more, something I had feared to find.

Armed with the volume, and the lemon forgotten—where the cook found it next day and made much of the mystery—I went upstairs again.

Viewed in a strong light, the three articles took on real significance. The spectacles I fancied were Miss Emily's. They were, to all appearances, the duplicates of those on her tidy bedside stand. But the handkerchief was not hers. Even without the scent, which had left it, but clung obstinately to the pages of the book, I knew it was not hers. It was florid, embroidered, and cheap. And held close to the light, I made out a laundry mark in ink on the border. The name was either *Wright* or *Knight*.

The notebook was an old one, and covered a period of almost twenty years. It contained dates and cash entries. The entries were nearly all in the Reverend Samuel Thaddeus's hand, but after the date of his death they had been continued in Miss Emily's writing. They varied little, save that the amounts gradually increased toward the end, and the dates were further apart. Thus, in 1898 there were six entries, aggregating five hundred dollars. In 1902-1903 there were no entries at all, but in 1904 there was a single memorandum of a thousand dollars. The entire amount must have been close to twenty-five thousand dollars. There was nothing to show whether it was money saved or money spent, money paid out or come in.

But across the years 1902 and 1903, the Reverend Thaddeus had written diagonally the word "Australia." There was a certain amount of enlightenment there. Carlo Benton had been in Australia during those years. In his *Fifty Years in Bolivar County*, the father had rather naïvely quoted a letter from Carlo Benton in Melbourne. A record, then, in all probability, of sums paid by this harassed old man to a worthless son.

Only the handkerchief refused to be accounted for.

I did not sleep that night. More and more, as I lay wide-eyed through the night, it seemed to me that Miss Emily must be helped, that she was drifting miserably out of life for need of a helping hand.

Once, toward morning, I dozed off, to waken in a state of terror that I recognized as a return of the old fear. But it left me soon, although I lay awake until morning.

That day I made two resolves—to send for Willie and to make a determined effort to see the night telephone operator. My letter to Willie off, I tried to fill the day until the hour when the night telephone operator was up and about, late in the afternoon.

The delay was simplified by the arrival of Mrs. Graves, in white silk gloves and a black cotton umbrella as a sunshade. She had lost her air of being afraid I might patronize her, and explained pantingly that she had come on an errand, not to call.

"I'm at my Christmas presents now," she said, "and I've fixed on a bedroom set for Miss Emily. I suppose you won't care if I go right up and measure the dresser-top, will you?" I took her up, and her sharp eyes roved over the stairs and the upper hall.

"That's where Carlo died," she said. "It's never been used since, unless you—" She paused, staring into Miss Emily's deserted bedroom. "It's a good thing I came," she said. "The eye's no use to trust to, especially for bureaus."

She looked around the room. There was, at that moment, something tender about her. She even lowered her voice and softened it. It took on, almost comically, the refinements of Miss Emily's own speech.

"Whose photograph is that?" she asked suddenly. "I don't know that I ever saw it before. But it looks familiar, too."

She reflected before it. It was clear that she felt a sort of resentment at not recognizing the young and smiling woman in the old walnut frame, but a moment later she was measuring the dresser-top, her mind set on Christmas benevolence.

However, before she went out, she paused near the photograph.

"It's queer," she said. "I've been in this room about a thousand times, and I've never noticed it before. I suppose you can get so accustomed to a thing that you don't notice it."

As she went out, she turned to me, and I gathered that not only the measurement for a gift had brought her that afternoon.

"About those books," she said. "I run on a lot when I get to talking. I suppose I shouldn't have mentioned them. But I'm sure you'll keep the story to yourself. I've never even told Mr. Graves."

"Of course I shall," I assured her. "But—didn't the hackman see you packing the books?"

"No, indeed. We packed them the afternoon after the funeral, and it was the next day that Staley took them off. He thought it was old bedding and so on, and he hinted to have it given to him. So Miss Emily and I went along to see it was done right."

So I discovered that the box had sat overnight in the Benton House. There remained, if I was to help Miss Emily, to discover what had occurred in those dark hours when the books were taken out and something else substituted.

The total result of my conversation that afternoon on the front porch of the small frame house on a side street with the night telephone operator was additional mystery.

I was not prepared for it. I had anticipated resentment and possibly insolence. But I had not expected to find fright. Yet the girl was undeniably frightened. I had hardly told her the object of my visit before I realized that she was in a state of almost panic.

"You can understand how I feel," I said. "I have no desire to report the matter, of course. But someone has been calling the house repeatedly at night, listening until I reply, and then hanging up the receiver. It is not accidental. It has happened too often."

"I'm not supposed to give out information about calls."

"But—just think a moment," I went on. "Suppose someone is planning to rob the house, and using this method of finding out if we are there or not?"

"I don't remember anything about the calls you are talking about," she parried, without looking at me. "As busy as I am—"

"Nonsense," I put in, "you know perfectly well what I am talking about. How do I know but that it is the intention of someone to lure me downstairs to the telephone and then murder me?"

"I am sure it is not that," she said. For almost the first time she looked directly at me, and I caught a flash of something—not defiance. It was, indeed, rather like reassurance.

"You see, you *know* it is not that." I felt all at once that she did know who was calling me at night, and why. And, moreover, that she would not tell. If, as I suspected, it was Miss Emily, this girl must be to some extent in her confidence.

"But—suppose for a moment that I think I know who is calling me?" I hesitated. She was a pretty girl, with an amiable face, and more than a suggestion of good breeding and intelligence about her. I made a

80

quick resolve to appeal to her. "My dear child," I said, "I want so very much, if I can, to help someone who is in trouble. But before I can help, I must know that I can help, and I must be sure it is necessary. I wonder if you know what I am talking about?"

"Why don't you go back to the city?" she said suddenly. "Go away and forget all about us here. That would help more than anything."

"But—would it?" I asked gently. "Would my going away help—her?"

To my absolute amazement she began to cry. We had been sitting on a cheap porch seat, side by side, and she turned her back to me and put her head against the arm of the bench. "She's going to die!" she said shakily. "She's weaker every day. She is slipping away, and no one does anything."

But I got nothing more from her. She had understood me, it was clear, and when at last she stopped crying, she knew well enough that she had betrayed her understanding. But she would not talk. I felt that she was not unfriendly, and that she was uncertain rather than stubborn. In the end I got up, little better off than when I came.

"I'll give you time to think it over," I said. "Not so much about the telephone calls, because you've really answered that. But about Miss Emily. She needs help, and I want to help her. But you tie my hands."

She had a sort of gift for silence. As I grew later on to know Anne Bullard better, I realized that even more. So now she sat silent, and let me talk.

"What I want," I said, "is to have Miss Emily know that I am friendly—that I am willing to do anything to—to show my friendliness. *Anything.*"

"You see," she said, with a kind of dogged patience, "it isn't really up to you, or to me either. It's something else." She hesitated. "She's very obstinate," she added.

When I went away I was aware that her eyes followed me, anxious and thoughtful eyes, with something of Miss Emily's own wide-eyed gaze.

Willie came late the next evening. I had indeed gone upstairs to retire when I heard his car in the drive. When I admitted him, he drew me into the library and gave me a good looking over.

"As I thought!" he said. "Nerves gone, looks gone. I told you Maggie would put a curse on you. What is it?"

So I told him. The telephone he already knew about. The confession he read over twice, and then observed, characteristically, that he would be eternally—I think the word is "Hornswoggled."

When I brought out *The Handwriting of God*, following Mrs. Graves's story of the books, he looked thoughtful. And indeed by the end of the recital he was very grave.

"Sprague is a lunatic," he said, with conviction. "There was a body, and it went into the river in the packing-case. It is distinctly possible that this Knight—or Wright—woman, who owned the handkerchief, was the victim. However, that's for later on. The plain truth is that there was a murder, and that

Miss Emily is shielding someone else."

And, after all, that was the only immediate result of Willie's visit—a new theory! So that now it stood: there was a crime. There was no crime. Miss Emily had committed it. Miss Emily had not committed it. Miss Emily had confessed it, but someone else had committed it.

For a few hours, however, our attention was distracted from Miss Emily and her concerns by the attempted robbery of the house that night. I knew nothing of it until I heard Willie shouting downstairs. I was deeply asleep, relaxed no doubt by the consciousness that at last there was a man in the house. And, indeed, Maggie slept for the same reason through the entire occurrence.

"Stop, or I'll fire!" Willie repeated, as I sat up in bed.

I knew quite well that he had no weapon. There was not one in the house. But the next moment there was a loud report, either a door slamming or a pistol shot, and I ran to the head of the stairs.

There was no light below, but a current of cool night air came up the staircase. And suddenly I realized that there was complete silence in the house.

"Willie!" I cried out, in an agony of fright. But he did not reply. And then, suddenly, the telephone rang.

I did not answer it. I know now why it rang, that there was real anxiety behind its summons. But I hardly heard it then. I was convinced that Willie had been shot.

I must have gone noiselessly down the stairs, and at the foot I ran directly into Willie. He was standing

83

there, only a deeper shadow in the blackness, and I had placed my hand over his, as it lay on the newel-post, before he knew I was on the staircase. He wheeled sharply, and I felt, to my surprise, that he held a revolver in his hand.

"Willie! What is it?" I said in a low tone.

"Sh," he whispered. "Don't move—or speak."

We listened, standing together. There was undoubtedly sounds outside, someone moving about, a hand on a window-catch, and finally not particularly cautious steps at the front door. It swung open. I could hear it creak as it moved slowly on its hinges.

I put a hand out to steady myself by the comfort of Willie's presence before me, between me and that softly opening door. But Willie was moving forward, crouched down, I fancied, and the memory of that revolver terrified me.

"Don't shoot him, Willie!" I almost shrieked.

"Shoot whom?" said Willie's cool voice, just inside the door.

I knew then, and I went sick all over. Somewhere in the hall between us crouched the man I had taken for Willie, crouched with a revolver in his right hand. The door was still open, I knew, and I could hear Willie fumbling on the hall stand for matches. I called out something incoherent about not striking a light, but Willie, whistling softly to show how cool he was, struck a match. It was followed instantly by a report, and I closed my eyes.

When I opened them, Willie was standing unhurt, staring over the burning match at the door, which was closed, and I knew that the report had been but the bang of the heavy door.

"What in blazes slammed that door?" he said.

"The burglar, or whatever he is," I said, my voice trembling in spite of me. "He was here, in front of me. I laid my hand on his. He had a revolver in it. When you opened the door, he slipped out past you."

Willie muttered something, and went toward the door. A moment later I was alone again, and the telephone was ringing. I felt my way back along the hall. I touched the cat, which had been sleeping on the telephone stand. He merely turned over.

I have tried, in living that night over again, to record things as they impressed me. For, after all, this is a narrative of motive rather than of incidents, of emotions as against deeds. But at the time, the brief conversation over the telephone seemed to me both horrible and unnatural.

From a great distance a woman's voice said, "Is anything wrong there?"

That was the first question, and I felt quite sure that it was the Bullard girl's voice. That is, looking back from the safety of the next day, I so decided. At the time I had no thought whatever.

"There is nothing wrong," I replied. I do not know why I said it. Surely there was enough wrong, with Willie chasing an armed intruder through the garden.

I thought the connection had been cut, for there was a buzzing on the wire. But a second or so later there came an entirely different voice, one I had never heard before, a plaintive voice, full, I thought, of tears.

"Oh, please," said this voice, "go out and look in your garden, or along the road. Please—quickly!"

"You will have to explain," I said impatiently. "Of course we will go and look, but who is it, and why—"

I was cut off there, definitely, and I could not get "central's" attention again.

Willie's voice from the veranda boomed through the lower floor. "This is I," he called. "No boiling water, please. I am coming in."

He went into the library and lighted a lamp. He was smiling when I entered, a reassuring smile, but rather a sheepish one, too.

"To think of letting him get by like that!" he said. "The cheapest kind of a trick. He had slammed the door before to make me think he had gone out, and all the time he was inside. And you—why didn't you scream?"

"I thought it was you," I told him.

The library was in chaos. Letters were lying about, papers, books. The drawer of the large desk-table in the center of the room had been drawn out and searched. *The History of Bolivar County,* for instance, was lying on the floor, face down, in a most ignoble position. In one place books had been taken from a recess by the fireplace, revealing a small wall cupboard behind. I had never known of the hiding-place, but a glance into it revealed only a bottle of red ink and the manuscript of a sermon on missions.

Standing in the disorder of the room, I told Willie about the telephone message. He listened attentively, and at first skeptically.

"Probably a ruse to get us out of the house, but coming a trifle late to be useful," was his comment.

But I had read distress in the second voice, and said so. At last he went to the telephone.

"I'll verify it," he explained. "If someone is really anxious, I'll get the car and take a scout around."

But he received no satisfaction from the Bullard girl, who, he reported, listened stoically and then said she was sorry, but she did not remember who had called. On his reminding her that she must have a record, she countered with the flat statement that there had been no call for us that night.

Willie looked thoughtful when he returned to the library. "There's a queer story back of all this," he said. "I think I'll get the car and scout around anyway."

"He is armed, Willie," I protested.

"He doesn't want to shoot me, or he could have done it," was his answer. "I'll just take a look around, and come back to report."

It was half-past three by the time he was ready to go. He was, as he observed, rather sketchily clad, but the night was warm. I saw him off, and locked the door behind him. Then I went into the library to wait and to put things to rights while I waited.

The dawn is early in August, and although it was not more than half-past four when Willie came back, it was about daylight by that time. I went to the door and watched him bring the car to a standstill. He shook his head when he saw me.

"Absolutely nothing," he said. "It was a ruse to get me out of the house, of course. I've run the whole way between here and town twice."

"But that could not have taken an hour," I protested.

"No," he said. "I met the doctor—what's his

name?—the local M.D. anyhow—footing it out of the village to a case, and I took him to his destination. He has a car, it seems, but it's out of order. Interesting old chap," he added, as I led the way into the house. "Didn't know me from Adam, but opened up when he found who I was."

I had prepared coffee and carried the tray to the library. While I lighted the lamp, he stood, whistling softly, and thoughtfully. At last he said:

"Look here, Aunt Agnes, I think I'm a good bit of a fool, but—some time this morning I wish you would call up Thomas Jenkins, on the Elmsburg road, and find out if anyone is sick there."

But when I stared at him, he only laughed sheepishly. "You can see how your suspicious disposition has undermined and ruined my once trusting nature," he scoffed.

He took his coffee and then, stripping off his ulster, departed for bed. I stopped to put away the coffee things, and, with Maggie in mind, to hang up his motor-coat. It was then that the flashlight fell out. I picked it up. It was shaped like a revolver.

I stopped in Willie's room on my way to my own, and held it out to him.

"Where did you get that?" I asked.

"Good heavens!" he said, raising himself on his elbow. "It belongs to the doctor. He gave it to me to examine the fan belt. I must have dropped it into my pocket."

And still I was nowhere. Suppose I had touched this flashlight at the foot of the stairs and mistaken it for a revolver. Suppose that the doctor, making his way toward the village and finding himself pursued, had faced about and pretended to be leaving it? Grant, in a word, that Doctor Lingard himself had been our night visitor—what then? Why had he done it? What of the telephone call urging me to search the road? Did someone realize what was happening, and take this method of warning us and sending us after the fugitive?

I knew the Thomas Jenkins farm on the Elmsburg road. I had, indeed, bought vegetables and eggs from Mr. Jenkins himself. That morning, as early as I dared, I called the Jenkins farm. Mr. Jenkins himself would bring me three dozen eggs that day. They were a little torn up out there, as Mrs. Jenkins had borne a small daughter at seven a.m.

When I told Willie, he was evidently relieved.

"I'm glad of it," he said heartily. "The doctor's a fine old chap, and I'd hate to think he was mixed up in any shady business."

He was insistent, that day, that I give up the house. He said it was not safe, and I was inclined to agree with him. But although I did not tell him of it, I had even more strongly than ever the impression that something must be done to help Miss Emily, and that I was the one who must do it.

Yet, in the broad light of day, with the sunshine pouring into the rooms, I was compelled to confess that Willie's theory was more than upheld by the facts. First of all was the character of Miss Emily as I read it, sternly conscientious, proud, and yet gentle. Second, there was the connection of the Bullard girl with the case. And third, there was the invader of the night before, an unknown quantity where so much seemed known, where a situation involving Miss Emily alone seemed to call for no one else.

Willie put the matter flatly to me as he stood in the hall, drawing on his gloves.

"Do you *want* to follow it up?" he asked. "Isn't it better to let it go? After all, you have only rented the house. You haven't taken over its history, or any responsibility but the rent."

"I think Miss Emily needs to be helped," I said, rather feebly.

"Let her friends help her. She has plenty of them. Besides, isn't it rather a queer way to help her, to try to fasten a murder on her?"

I could not explain what I felt so strongly—that Miss Emily could only be helped by being hurt, that whatever she was concealing, the long concealment was killing her. That I felt in her—it is always difficult to put what I felt about Miss Emily into words—both hoped for and dreaded desperately the light of the truth.

But if I was hardly practical when it came to Miss Emily, I was rational enough in other things. It is with no small pride—but without exultation, for in the end it cost too much—that I point to the solution of one issue as my own.

With Willie gone, Maggie and I settled down to the quiet tenure of our days. She informed me, on the morning after that eventful night, that she had not closed an eye after one o'clock! She came into the library and asked me if I could order her some sleeping-powders.

"Fiddlesticks!" I said sharply. "You slept all

night. I was up and around the house, and you never knew it."

"Honest to heaven, Miss Agnes, I never slep' at all. I heard a horse gallopin', like it was runnin' off, and it waked me for good."

And after a time I felt that, however mistaken Maggie had been about her night's sleep, she was possibly correct about the horse.

"He started to run about the stable somewhere," she said. "You can smile if you want. That's the heaven's truth. And he came down the drive on the jump and out onto the road."

"We can go and look for hoof marks," I said and rose. But Maggie only shook her head.

"It was no real horse, Miss Agnes," she said. "You'll find nothing. Anyhow, I've been and looked. There's not a mark."

But Maggie was wrong. I found hoofprints in plenty in the turf beside the drive, and a track of them through the lettuce-bed in the garden. More than that, behind the stable I found where a horse had been tied and had broken away. A piece of worn strap still hung there. It was sufficiently clear, then, that whoever had broken into the house had come on horseback and left afoot. But many people in the neighborhood used horses. The clue, if clue it can be called, got me nowhere.

Chapter 4

For several days things remained *in statu quo*. Our lives went on evenly. The telephone was at our service, without any of its past vagaries. Maggie's eyes ceased to look as if they were being pushed out from behind, and I ceased to waken at night and listen for untoward signs.

Willie telephoned daily. He was frankly uneasy about my remaining there. "You know something that somebody resents your knowing," he said, a day or two after the night visitor. "It may become very uncomfortable for you."

And, after a day or two, I began to feel that it was being made uncomfortable for me. I am a social being; I like people. In the city my neighborly instincts have died of a sort of brick-wall apathy, but in the country it comes to life again. The instinct of gregariousness is as old as the first hamlets, I dare say, when prehistoric man ceased to live in trees, and banded together for protection from the wild beasts that walked the earth.

The village became unfriendly. It was almost a matter of a night. One day the postmistress leaned on the shelf at her window and chatted with me. The next she passed out my letters with hardly a glance. Mrs. Graves did not see me at early communion on Sunday morning. The hackman was busy when I called him. It was intangible, a matter of omission, not commission. The doctor's wife, who had asked me to tea, called up and regretted that she must go to the city that day.

I sat down then and took stock of things. Did the village believe that Miss Emily must be saved from me? Did the village know the story I was trying to learn, and was it determined I should never find out the truth? And, if this was so, was the village right or was I? They would save Miss Emily by concealment, while I felt that concealment had failed, and that only the truth would do. Did the village know, or only suspect? Or was it not the village at all, but one or two people who were determined to drive me away?

My theories were rudely disturbed shortly after that by a visit from Martin Sprague. I fancied that Willie had sent him, but he evaded my question.

"I'd like another look at the slip of paper," he said. "Where do you keep it, by the way?"

"In a safe place," I replied noncommittally, and he laughed. The truth was that I had taken out the removable inner sole of a slipper and had placed it underneath, an excellent hiding-place, but one I did not care to confide to him. When I had brought it downstairs, he read it over again carefully, and then sat back with it in his hand.

"Now tell me about everything," he said.

I did, while he listened attentively. Afterward we walked back to the barn, and I showed him the piece of broken halter still tied there.

He surveyed it without comment, but on the way back to the house he said: "If the village is lined up as you say it is, I suppose it is useless to interview the harnessmaker. He has probably repaired that strap, or sold a new one, to whoever— It would be a nice clue to follow up."

"I am not doing detective work," I said shortly. "I am trying to help someone who is dying of anxiety and terror."

He nodded. "I get you," he said. But his tone was not flippant. "The fact is, of course, that the early theory won't hold. There has been a crime, and the little old lady did not commit it. But suppose you find out who did it. How is that going to help her?"

"I don't know, Martin," I said, in a sort of desperation. "But I have the most curious feeling that she is depending on me. The way she spoke the day I saw her, and her eyes and everything; I know you think it nonsense," I finished lamely.

"I think you'd better give up the place and go back to town," he said. But I saw that he watched me carefully, and when at last he got up to go, he put a hand on my shoulder.

"I think you are right, after all," he said. "There are a good many things that can't be reasoned out with any logic we have, but that are true, nevertheless. We call it intuition, but it's really subconscious intelligence. Stay, by all means, if you feel you should."

In the doorway he said, "Remember this, Miss Agnes. Both a crime of violence and a confession like the one in your hand are the products of impulse. They are not, either of them, premeditated. They are not the work, then, of a calculating or cautious nature. Look for a big, emotional type."

It was a day or two after that that I made my visit to Miss Emily. I had stopped once before, to be told with an air of finality that the invalid was asleep. On this occasion I took with me a basket of fruit. I had half expected a refusal, but I was admitted.

The Bullard girl was with Miss Emily. She had, I think, been kneeling beside the bed, and her eyes were red and swollen. But Miss Emily herself was as cool, as dainty and starched and fragile as ever. More so, I thought. She was thinner, and although it was a warm August day, a white silk shawl was wrapped around her shoulders and fastened with an amethyst brooch. In my clasp her thin hand felt hot and dry.

"I have been waiting for you," she said simply.

She looked at Anne Bullard, and the message in her eyes was plain enough. But the girl ignored it. She stood across the bed from me and eyed me steadily.

"My dear," said Miss Emily, in her high-bred voice, "if you have anything to do, Miss Blakiston will sit with me for a little while."

"I have nothing to do," said the girl doggedly. Perhaps this is not the word. She had more the look of endurance and supreme patience. There was no sharpness about her, although there was vigilance.

Miss Emily sighed, and I saw her eyes seek the

Bible beside her. But she only said gently. "Then sit down, dear. You can work at my knitting if you like. My hands get very tired."

She asked me questions about the house and the garden. The raspberries were usually quite good, and she was rather celebrated for her lettuce. If I had more than I needed, would I mind if Mr. Staley took a few in to the doctor, who was fond of them.

The mention of Doctor Lingard took me back to the night of the burglary. I wondered if to tell Miss Emily would unduly agitate her. I think I would not have told her, but I caught the girl's eye, across the bed, raised from her knitting and fixed on me with a peculiar intensity. Suddenly it seemed to me that Miss Emily was surrounded by a conspiracy of silence, and it roused my antagonism.

"There are plenty of lettuces," I said, "although a few were trampled by a runaway horse the other night. It is rather a curious story."

So I told her of our night visitor. I told it humorously, lightly, touching on my own horror at finding I had been standing with my hand on the burglar's shoulder. But I was sorry for my impulse immediately, for I saw Miss Emily's body grow rigid, and her hands twist together. She did not look at me. She stared fixedly at the girl. Their eyes met.

It was as if Miss Emily asked a question which the girl refused to answer. It was as certain as though it had been a matter of words instead of glances. It was over in a moment. Miss Bullard went back to her knitting, but Miss Emily lay still.

"I think I should not have told you," I apologized. "I thought it might interest you. Of course nothing whatever was taken, and no damage done—except to the lettuce."

"Anne," said Miss Emily, "will you bring me some fresh water?"

The girl rose reluctantly, but she did not go farther than the top of the staircase, just beyond the door. We heard her calling to someone below, in her clear young voice, to bring the water, and the next moment she was back in the room. But Miss Emily had had the opportunity for one sentence.

"I know now," she said quietly, "that you have found it."

Anne Bullard was watching from the doorway, and it seemed to me, having got so far, I could not retreat. I must go on.

"Miss Bullard," I said, "I would like to have just a short conversation with Miss Emily. It is about a private matter. I am sure you will not mind if I ask you—"

"I shall not go out."

"Anne!" said Miss Emily sharply.

The girl was dogged enough by that time. Both dogged and frightened, I felt. But she stood her ground.

"She is not to be worried about anything," she insisted. "And she's not supposed to have visitors. That's the doctor's orders."

I felt outraged and indignant, but against the stone wall of the girl's presence and her distrust I was helpless. I got up, with as much dignity as I could muster.

"I should have been told that downstairs."

"The woman's a fool," said Anne Bullard, with a

sort of suppressed fierceness. She stood aside as, having said good-by to Miss Emily, I went out, and I felt that she hardly breathed until I had got safely to the street.

Looking back, I feel that Emily Benton died at the hands of her friends. For she died, indeed, died in the act of trying to tell me what they had determined she should never tell. Died of kindness and misunderstanding. Died repressed, as she had lived repressed. Yet, I think, died calmly and bravely.

I made no further attempt to see her, and Maggie and I took up again the quiet course of our lives. The telephone did not ring of nights. The cat came and went, spending its days with Miss Emily and its nights with us. I have wondered since how many nights Miss Emily had spent in the low chair in that back hall, where the confession lay hidden, that the cat should feel it could sleep nowhere else.

The days went by, warm days and cooler ones, but rarely rainy ones. The dust from the road settled thick over flowers and shrubbery. The lettuce wilted, and those that stood up in the sun were strong and bitter. By the end of August we were gasping in a hot dryness that cracked the skin and made any but cold food impossible.

Miss Emily lay through it all in her hot upper room in the village, and my attempt, through Doctor Lingard, to coax her back to the house by offering to leave it brought only a negative.

"It would be better for her, you understand," the doctor said, over the telephone. "But she is very determined, and she insists on remaining where she is."

And I believe this was the truth. They would surely have been glad to get rid of me, these friends of Miss Emily's.

I have wondered since what they thought of me, Anne Bullard and the doctor, to have feared me as they did. I look in the mirror, and I see a middle-aged woman, with a determined nose, slightly inquisitive, and what I trust is a humorous mouth, for it has no other virtues. But they feared me. Perhaps long looking for a danger affects the mental vision. Anyhow, by the doctor's order, I was not allowed to call and see Miss Emily again.

Then, one night, the heat suddenly lifted. One moment I was sitting on the veranda, lifeless and inert, and the next a cool wind, with a hint of rain, had set the shutters to banging and the curtains to flowing, like flags of truce, from the windows. The air was life, energy. I felt revivified.

And something of the same sort must have happened to Miss Emily. She must have sat up among her pillows, her face fanned with the electric breeze, and made her determination to see me. Ann Bullard was at work, and she was free from observation.

It must have been nine o'clock when she left the house, a shaken little figure in black, not as neat as usual, but hooked and buttoned, for all that, with no one will ever know what agony of old hands.

She was two hours and a half getting to the house, and the rain came at ten o'clock. By half after eleven, when the doorbell rang, she was a sodden mass of wet garments, and her teeth were chattering when I led her into the library.

She could not talk. The thing she had come to say was totally beyond her. I put her to bed in her own room. And two days later she died.

I made no protest when Anne Bullard presented herself at the door the morning after Miss Emily arrived, and, walking into the house, took sleepless charge of the sickroom. And I made no reference save once to the reason for the tragedy. That was the night Miss Emily died.

Anne Bullard had called to me that she feared there was a change, and I went into the sickroom. There was a change, and I could only shake my head. She burst out at me then.

"If only you had never taken this house!" she said. "You people with money, you think there is nothing you can not have. You came, and now look!"

"Anne," I said with a bitterness I could not conceal, "Miss Emily is not young, and I think she is ready to go. But she has been killed by her friends. I wanted to help, but they would not allow me to."

Toward morning there was nothing more to be done, and we sat together, listening to the stertorous breathing from the bed. Maggie, who had been up all night, had given me notice at three in the morning, and was upstairs packing her trunk.

I went into my room, and brought back Miss Emily's confession.

"Isn't it time," I said, "to tell me about this? I ought to know, I think, before she goes. If it is not true, you owe it to her, I think." But she shook her head.

I looked at the confession, and from it to Miss Emily's pinched old face.

To whom it may concern: On the 30th day of May, 1911, I killed a woman here in this house. I hope you will not find this until I am dead.
(Signed) EMILY BENTON

Anne was watching me. I went to the mantel and got a match, and then, standing near the bed, I lighted it and touched it to the paper. It burned slowly, a thin blue semicircle of fire that ate its way slowly across until there was but the corner I held. I dropped it into the fireplace and watched it turn to black ash.

I may have fancied it—I am always fancying things about Miss Emily—but I will always think that she knew. She drew a longer, quieter breath, and her eyes, fixed and staring, closed. I think she died in the first sleep she had had in twenty-four hours.

I had expected Anne Bullard to show emotion, for no one could doubt her attachment to Miss Emily. But she only stood stoically by the bed for a moment and then, turning swiftly, went to the wall opposite and took down from the wall the walnut-framed photograph Mrs. Graves had commented on.

Anne Bullard stood with the picture in her hand, looking at it. And suddenly she broke into sobs. It was stormy weeping, and I got the impression that she wept, not for Miss Emily, but for many other things,—as though the piled-up grief of years had broken out at last.

She took the photograph away, and I never saw it again.

Miss Emily was buried from her home. I obliterated myself, and her friends, who were, I felt, her murderers, came in and took charge. They paid me the tribute of much politeness, but no cordiality, and I think they felt toward me as I felt toward them. They blamed me with the whole affair.

She left her property all to Anne Bullard, to the astonished rage of the congregation, which had expected the return of its dimes and quarters, no doubt, in the shape of a new altar, or perhaps an organ.

"Not a cent to keep up the mausoleum or anything," Mrs. Graves confided to me. "And nothing to the church. All to that telephone girl, who comes from no one knows where! It's enough to make her father turn over in his grave. It has set people talking, I can tell you."

Maggie's mental state during the days preceding the funeral was curious. She coupled the most meticulous care as to the preparations for the ceremony, and a sort of loving gentleness when she decked Miss Emily's small old frame for its last rites, with suspicion and hatred of Miss Emily living. And this suspicion she held also against Anne Bullard.

Yet she did not want to leave the house. I do not know just what she expected to find. We were cleaning up preparatory to going back to the city, and I felt that at least a part of Maggie's enthusiasm for corners was due to a hope of locating more concealed papers. She was rather less than polite to the Bullard girl, who was staying on at my invitation—because the village was now flagrantly unfriendly and suspicious of her. And for some strange reason, the fact that Miss Emily's cat followed Anne everywhere convinced Maggie that her suspicions were justified.

"It's like this, Miss Agnes," she said one morning, leaning on the handle of a floor brush. "She had some power over the old lady, and that's how she got the property. And I am saying nothing, but she's no Christian, that girl. To see her and that cat going out night after night, both snooping along on their tiptoes—it ain't normal."

I had several visits from Martin Sprague since Miss Emily's death, and after a time I realized that he was interested in Anne. She was quite attractive in her mourning clothes, and there was something about her, not in feature, but in neatness and in the way her things had of, well, staying in place, that reminded me of Miss Emily herself. It was rather surprising, too, to see the way she fitted into her new surroundings and circumstances.

But I did not approve of Martin's attraction to her. She had volunteered no information about herself; she apparently had no people. She was a lady, I felt, although, with the exception of her new mourning, her clothing was shabby and her linen even coarse.

She held the key to the confession. I knew that. And I had no more hope of getting it from her than I had from the cat. So I prepared to go back to the city, with the mystery unsolved. It seemed a pity, when I had got so far with it. I had reconstructed a situation out of such bricks as I had, the books in the cellar, Mrs. Graves's story of the river, the confession, possibly the notebook and the handkerchief. I had even some material left over in the form of the night intruder, who may or may not have been the doctor. And then, having got so far, I had had to stop for lack of other bricks.

A day or two before I went back to the city, Maggie came to me with a folded handkerchief in her hand.

"Is that yours?" she asked.

I disclaimed it. It was not very fine, and looked rather yellow.

"S'got a name on it," Maggie volunteered. "Wright, I think it is. 'Tain't hers, unless she's picked it up somewhere. It's just come out of the wash."

Maggie's eyes were snapping with suspicion. "There ain't any Wrights around here, Miss Agnes," she said. "I sh'd say she's here under a false name. Wright's likely hers."

In tracing the mystery of the confession, I find that three apparently disconnected discoveries paved the way to its solution. Of these the handkerchief came first.

I was inclined to think that in some manner the handkerchief I had found in the book in the cellar had got into the wash. But it was where I had placed it for safety, in the wall closet in the library. I brought it out and compared the two. They were unlike, save in one regard. The name *Wright* was clear enough on the one Maggie had found. With it as a guide, the other name was easily seen to be the same. Moreover, both had been marked by the same hand.

Yet, on Anne Bullard being shown the one Maggie had found, she disclaimed it. "Don't you think someone dropped it at the funeral?" she asked.

But I thought, as I turned away, that she took a step toward me. When I stopped, however, and faced about, she was intent on something outside the window.

And so it went. I got nowhere. And now, by way of complication, I felt my sympathy for Anne's loneliness turning to genuine interest. She was so stoical, so repressed, and so lonely. And she was tremendously proud. Her pride was vaguely reminiscent of Miss Emily's. She bore her ostracism almost fiercely, yet there were times when I felt her eyes on me, singularly gentle and appealing. Yet she volunteered nothing about herself.

I intended to finish the history of Bolivar County before I left. I dislike not finishing a book. Besides, this one fascinated me—the smug complacence and almost loud virtue of the author, his satisfaction in Bolivar County, and his small hits at the world outside, his patronage to those not of it. And always, when I began to read, I turned to the inscription in Miss Emily's hand, the hand of the confession—and I wondered if she had really believed it all.

So on this day I found the name Bullard in the book. It had belonged to the Reverend Samuel Thaddeus's grandmother, and he distinctly stated that she was the last of her line. He inferred indeed, that since the line was to end, it had chosen a fitting finish in his immediate progenitor.

That night, at dinner, I said, "Anne, are there any Bullards in this neighborhood now?"

"I have never heard of any. But I have not been here long."

"It is not a common name," I persisted.

But she received my statement in silence. She had, as I have said, rather a gift for silence.

That afternoon I was wandering about the garden

snipping faded roses with Miss Emily's garden shears, when I saw Maggie coming swiftly toward me. When she caught my eye, she beckoned to me. "Walk quiet, Miss Agnes," she said, "and don't say I didn't warn you. She's in the library."

So, feeling hatefuly like a spy, I went quietly over the lawn toward the library windows. They were long ones, to the floor, and at first I made out nothing. Then I saw Anne. She was on her knees, following the border of the carpet with fingers that examined it, inch by inch.

She turned, as if she felt our eyes on her, and saw us. I shall never forget her face. She looked stricken. I turned away. There was something in her eyes that made me think of Miss Emily, lying among her pillows and waiting for me to say the thing she was dreading to hear.

I sent Maggie away with a gesture. There was something in her pursed lips that threatened danger. For I felt then as if I had always known it and only just realized I knew it, that somewhere in that room lay the answer to all questions; lay Miss Emily's secret. And I did not wish to learn it. It was better to go on wondering, to question and doubt and decide and decide again. I was, I think, in a state of nervous terror by that time, terror and apprehension.

While Miss Emily lived, I had hoped to help. But now it seemed too hatefully like accusing when she could not defend herself. And there is another element that I am bound to acknowledge. There was an element of jealousy of Anne Bullard. Both of us had tried to help Miss Emily. She had foiled my attempt in her own endeavor, a mistaken endeavor, I felt. But there was now to be no blemish on my efforts. I would no longer pry or question or watch. It was too late.

In a curious fashion, each of us wished, I think, to prove the quality of her tenderness for the little old lady who was gone beyond all human tenderness.

So that evening, after dinner, I faced Anne in the library.

"Why not let things be as they are, Anne?" I asked. "It can do no good. Whatever it is, and I do not know, why not let things rest?"

"Someone may find it," she replied. "Someone who does not care, as I—as we care."

"Are you sure there is something?"

"She told me, near the last. I only don't know just where it is."

"And if you find it?"

"It is a letter. I shall burn it without reading. Although," she drew a long breath, "I know what it contains."

"If in any way it comes into my hands," I assured her, "I shall let you know. And I shall not read it."

She looked thoughtful rather than grateful.

"I hardly know," she said. "I think she would want you to read it if it came to you. It explains so much. And it was a part of her plan. You know, of course, that she had a plan. It was a sort of arrangement"— she hesitated—"it was a sort of pact she made with God, if you know what I mean."

That night Maggie found the letter.

I had gone upstairs, and Anne was, I think, already

asleep. I heard what sounded like distant hammering, and I went to the door. Someone was in the library below. The light was shining out into the hall, and my discovery of that was followed almost immediately by the faint splintering of wood. Rather outraged than alarmed, I went back for my dressing-gown, and as I left the room, I confronted Maggie in the hallway. She had an envelope in one hand, and a hatchet in the other.

"I found it," she said briefly.

She held it out, and I took it. On the outside, in Miss Emily's writing, it said, *To whom it may concern*. It was sealed.

I turned it over in my hand, while Maggie talked.

"When I saw that girl crawling around," she said, "seems to me I remembered all at once seeing Miss Emily, that day I found her, running her finger along the baseboard. Says I to myself, there's something more hidden, and she don't know where it is. But I do. So I lifted the baseboard, and this was behind it."

Anne heard her from her room, and she went out soon afterward. I heard her going down the stairs and called to her. But she did not answer. I closed the door on Maggie and stood in my room, staring at the envelope.

I have wondered since whether Miss Emily, had she lived, would have put the responsibility on Providence for the discovery of her pitiful story. So many of us blame the remorseless hand of destiny for what is so manifestly our own doing. It was her own anxiety, surely, that led to the discovery in each instance, yet I am certain that old Emily Benton died convinced that a higher hand than any on earth had directed the discovery of the confession.

Miss Emily has been dead for more than a year now. To publish the letter can do her no harm. In a way, too, I feel, it may be the fulfillment of that strange pact she made. For just as discovery was the thing she most dreaded, so she felt that by paying her penalty here she would be saved something beyond— that sort of spiritual bookkeeping which most of us call religion.

Anne Sprague—she is married now to Martin— has, I think, some of Miss Emily's feeling about it, although she denies it. But I am sure that in consenting to the recording of Miss Emily's story, she feels that she is doing what that gentle fatalist would call following the hand of Providence.

I read the letter that night in the library, where the light was good. It was a narrative, not a letter, strictly speaking. It began abruptly.

I must set down this thing as it happened. I shall write it fully, because I must get it off my mind. I find that I am always composing it, and that my lips move when I walk along the street or even when I am sitting in church. How terrible if I should some day speak it aloud. My great-grandmother was a Catholic. She was a Bullard. Perhaps it is from her that I have this overwhelming impulse to confession. And lately I have been terrified. I must tell it, or I shall shriek it out some day, in the church, during the Litany. "From battle and murder, and from sudden death, Good Lord, deliver us."

(There was a space here. When the writing began again, time had elapsed. The ink was different, the writing more controlled.)

What a terrible thing hate is. It is a poison. It penetrates the mind and the body and changes everything. I, who once thought I could hate no one, now find that hate is my daily life, my getting up and lying down, my sleep, my waking.

"From hatred, envy, and malice, and all uncharitableness, Good Lord, deliver us."

Must one suffer twice for the same thing? Is it not true that we pay but one penalty? Surely we pay either here or beyond, but not both. Oh, not both!

Will this ever be found? Where shall I hide it? For I have the feeling that I must hide it, not destroy it—as the Catholic buries his sin with the priest. My father once said that it is the healthful humiliation of the confessional that is its reason for existing. If humiliation be a virtue—

I have copied the confession to this point, but I find I can not go on. She was so merciless to herself, so hideously calm, so exact as to dates and hours. She had laid her life on the table and dissected it—for the Almighty!

110

I heard the story that night gently told, and somehow I feel that that is the version by which Miss Emily will be judged.

"If humiliation be a virtue—" I read and was about to turn the page, when I heard Anne in the hall. She was not alone. I recognized Doctor Lingard's voice.

Five minutes later I was sitting opposite him, almost knee to knee, and he was telling me how Miss Emily had come to commit her crime. Anne Bullard was there, standing on the hearth rug. She kept her eyes on me, and after a time I realized that these two simple people feared me, feared for Miss Emily's gentle memory, feared that I—good heaven!—would make the thing public.

"First of all, Miss Blakiston," said the doctor, "one must have known the family to realize the situation—its pride in its own uprightness. The virtue of the name, what it stood for in Bolivar County. She was raised on that. A Benton could do no wrong, because a Benton would do no wrong.

"But there is another side also. I doubt if any girl was ever raised as Miss Emily was. She—well, she knew nothing. At fifty she was as childlike and innocent as she was at ten. She had practically never heard of vice. The ugly things, for her, did not exist.

"And, all the time, there was a deep and strong nature underneath. She should have married and had children, but there was no one here for her to marry. I," he smiled faintly, "I asked for her myself, and was forbidden the house for years as a result.

"You have heard of the brother? But of course you have. I know you have found the books. Such an existence as the family life here was bound to have its

111

reactions. Carlo was a reaction. Twenty-five years ago he ran away with a girl from the village. He did not marry her. I believe he was willing at one time, but his father opposed it violently. It would have been to recognize a thing he refused to recognize." He turned suddenly to Anne. "Don't you think this is going to be painful?" he asked.

"Why? I know it all."

"Very well. This girl—the one Carlo ran away with—determined to make the family pay for that refusal. She made them actually pay, year by year. Emily knew about it. She had to pinch to make the payments. The father sat in a sort of detached position, in the center of Bolivar County, and let her bear the brunt of it. I shall never forget the day she learned there was a child. It—well, it sickened her. She had not known about those things. And I imagine, if we could know, that that was the beginning of things.

"And all the time there was the necessity for secrecy. She had never known deceit, and now she was obliged to practice it constantly. She had no one to talk to. Her father, beyond making entries of the amounts paid to the woman in the case, had nothing to do with it. She bore it all, year after year. And it ate, like a cancer.

"Remember, I never knew. I, who would have done anything for her—she never told me. Carlo lived hard and came back to die. The father went. She nursed them both. I came every day, and I never suspected. Only, now and then, I wondered about her. She looked *burned*. I don't know any other word.

"Then, the night after Carlo had been buried, she

telephoned for me. It was eleven o'clock. She met me, out there in the hall, and she said, 'John, I have killed somebody.'

"I thought she was out of her mind. But she opened the door, and—"

He turned and glanced at Anne.

"Please!" she said.

"It was Anne's mother. You have guessed it about Anne by now, of course. It seems that the funeral had taken the money for the payment that was due, and there had been a threat of exposure. And Emily had reached the breaking-point. I believe what she said— that she had no intention even of striking her. You can't take the act itself. You have to take twenty-five years into account. Anyhow, she picked up a chair and knocked the woman down. And it killed her." He ran his fingers through his heavy hair. "It should not have killed her," he reflected. "There must have been some other weakness, heart or something. I don't know. But it was a heavy chair. I don't see how Emily—"

His voice trailed off.

"There we were," he said, with a long breath. "Poor Emily, and the other poor soul, neither of them fundamentally at fault, both victims."

"I know about the books," I put in hastily. I could not have him going over that again.

"You knew that, too!" He gazed at me.

"Poor Emily," he said. "She tried to atone. She brought Anne here, and told her the whole story. It was a bad time—all around. But at last Anne saw the light. The only one who would not see the light was Emily. And at last she hit on this confession idea. I

113

suspected it when she rented the house. When I accused her of it, she said: 'I have given it to Providence to decide. If the confession is found, I shall know I am to suffer. And I shall not lift a hand to save myself.'"

So it went through the hours. Her fear, which I still think was the terror that communicated itself to me; the various clues, which she, poor victim, had overlooked; the articles laid carelessly in the book she had been reading and accidentally hidden with her brother's forbidden literature; the books themselves, with all of five years to destroy them, and left untouched; her own anxiety about the confession in the telephone-box, which led to our finding it; her espionage of the house by means of the telephone; the doctor's night visit in search of the confession; the daily penance for five years of the dead woman's photograph in her room—all of these—and her occasional weakenings, poor soul, when she tried to change her handwriting against discovery, and refused to allow the second telephone to be installed.

How clear it was! How, in a way, inevitable! And, too, how really best for her it had turned out. For she had made a pact, and she died believing that discovery here had come, and would take the place of punishment beyond.

Martin Sprague came the next day. I was in the library alone, and he was with Anne in the garden, when Maggie came into the room with a saucer of crab-apple jelly.

"I wish you'd look at this," she said. "If it's cooked

114

too much, it gets tough and—" She straightened suddenly and stood staring out through a window.

"I'd thank you to look out and see the goings on in our garden," she said sharply. "In broad daylight, too. I—"

But I did not hear what else Maggie had to say. I glanced out, and Martin had raised the girl's face to his and was kissing her, gently and very tenderly.

And then—and again, as with fear, it is hard to put into words—I felt come over me such a wave of contentment and happiness as made me close my eyes with the sheer relief and joy of it. All was well. The past was past, and out of its mistakes had come a beautiful thing. And, like the fear, this joy was not mine. It came to me. I picked it up—a thought without words.

Sometimes I think about it, and I wonder—did little Miss Emily know?

Sight Unseen

Chapter 1

The rather extraordinary story revealed by the experiments of the Neighborhood Club have been until now a matter only of private record. But it seems to me, as an active participant in the investigations, that they should be given to the public; not so much for what they will add to the existing data on psychical research, for from that angle they were not unusual, but as yet another exploration into that uncharted territory, the human mind.

The psychoanalysts have taught us something about the individual mind. They have their own patter, of complexes and primal instincts, of the unconscious, which is a sort of bonded warehouse from which we clandestinely withdraw our stored thoughts and impressions. They lay to this unconscious mind of ours all phenomena that cannot otherwise be labeled, and ascribe such demonstrations of power as cannot thus be explained to trickery, to black silk threads and folding rods, to slates with false sides and a medium with chalk on his finger nail.

In other words, they give us subjective mind but never objective mind. They take the mind and its reactions on itself and on the body. But what about objective mind? Does it make its only outward manifestations through speech and action? Can we ignore the effect of mind on mind, when there are present none of the ordinary media of communication? I think not.

In making the following statement concerning our part in the strange case of Arthur Wells, a certain allowance must be made for our ignorance of so-called psychic phenomena, and also for the fact that since that time, great advances have been made in scientific methods of investigation. For instance, we did not place Miss Jeremy's chair on a scale, to measure for any loss of weight. Also the theory or rods of invisible matter emanating from the medium's body, to move bodies at a distance from her, had only been evolved; and none of the methods for calculation of leverages and strains had been formulated, so far as I know.

To be frank, I am quite convinced that, even had we known of these so-called explanations, which in reality explain nothing, we would have ignored them as we became involved in the dramatic movement of the revelations and the personal experiences which grew out of them. I confess that following the night after the first seance any observations of mine would have been of no scientific value whatever, and I believe I can speak for the others also.

120

Of the medium herself I can only say that we have never questioned her integrity. The physical phenomena occurred before she went into trance, and during that time her forearms were rigid. During the deep trance, with which this unusual record deals, she spoke in her own voice, but in a querulous tone, and Sperry's examination of her pulse showed that it went from eighty normal to a hundred and twenty and very feeble.

With this preface I come to the death of Arthur Wells, our acquaintance and neighbor, and the investigation into that death by a group of six earnest people who call themselves the Neighborhood Club.

The Neighborhood Club was organized in my house. It was too small really to be called a club, but women have a way these days of conferring a titular dignity on their activities, and it is not so bad, after all. The Neighborhood Club it really was, composed of four of our neighbors, my wife, and myself.

We had drifted into the habit of dining together on Monday evenings at the different houses. There were Herbert Robinson and his sister Alice—not a young woman, but clever, alert, and very alive; Sperry, the well-known heart specialist, a bachelor still in spite of much feminine activity; and there was old Mrs. Dane, hopelessly crippled as to the knees with rheumatism, but one of those glowing and kindly souls that have a way of being a neighborhood nucleus. It was around her that we first gathered, with an idea of forming for her certain contact points with the active life from which she was otherwise cut off. But she gave us, I am sure, more than we brought her, and, as will be seen later, her shrewdness was an important element in solving our mystery.

In addition to these four there were my wife and myself.

It had been our policy to take up different subjects for these neighborhood dinners. Sperry was a reformer in his way, and on his nights we generally took up civic questions. He was particularly interested in the responsibility of the state to the sick poor. My wife and I had "political" evenings. Not really politics, except in their relation to life. I am a lawyer by profession, and dabble a bit in city government. The Robinsons had literature.

Don't misunderstand me. We had no papers, no set programs. On the Robinson evenings we discussed editorials and current periodicals, as well as the new books and plays. We were frequently acrimonious, I fear, but our small wrangles ended with the evening. Robinson was the literary editor of a paper, and his sister read for a large publishing house.

Mrs. Dane was a free-lance. "Give me that privilege," she begged. "At least, until you find my evenings dull. It gives me, during all the week before you come, a sort of thrilling feeling that the world is mine to choose from." The result was never dull. She led us all the way from moving-pictures to modern dress. She led us even further, as you will see.

On consulting my note-book I find that the first evening which directly concerns the Arthur Wells case was Monday, November the second.

It was a curious day, to begin with. There come days, now and then, that bring with them a strange sort of mental excitement. I have never analyzed them. With me on this occasion it took the form of nervous irritability, and something of apprehension. My wife, I remember, complained of headache, and one of the stenographers had a fainting attack.

I have often wondered for how much of what happened to Arthur Wells the day was responsible. There are days when the world is a place for love and play and laughter. And then there are sinister days, when the earth is a hideous place, when ever the thought of immortality is unbearable, and life itself a burden; when all that is riotous and unlawful comes forth and bares itself to the light.

This was such a day.

I am fond of my friends, but I found no pleasure in the thought of meeting them that evening. I remembered the odious squeak in the wheels of Mrs. Dane's chair. I resented the way Sperry would clear his throat. I read in the morning paper Herbert Robinson's review of a book I had liked, and disagreed with him. Disagreed violently. I wanted to call him on the telephone and tell him that he was a fool. I felt old, although I am only fifty-three, old and bitter, and tired.

With the fall of twilight, things changed somewhat. I was more passive. Wretchedness encompassed me, but I was not wretched. There was violence in the air, but I was not violent. And with a bath and my dinner clothes I put away the horrors of the day.

My wife was better, but the cook had given notice. "There has been quarreling among the servants all day," my wife said. "I wish I could go and live on a desert island."

We have no children, and my wife, for lack of other interest, finds her housekeeping an engrossing and serious matter. She is in the habit of bringing her domestic difficulties to me when I reach home in the evenings, a habit which sometimes renders me unjustly indignant. Most unjustly, for she has borne with me for thirty years and is known throughout the entire neighborhood as a perfect housekeeper. I can close my eyes and find any desired article in my bedroom at any time.

We passed the Wellses' house on our way to Mrs. Dane's that night, and my wife commented on the dark condition of the lower floor.

"Even if they are going out," she said, "it would add to the appearance of the street to leave a light or two burning. But some people have no public feeling."

I made no comment, I believe. The Wellses were a young couple, with children, and had been known to observe that they considered the neighborhood "stodgy." And we had retaliated, I regret to say, in kind, but not with any real unkindness, by regarding them as interlopers. They drove too many cars, and drove them too fast; they kept a governess and didn't see enough of their children; and their English butler made our neat maids look commonplace.

There is generally, in every old neighborhood, some one house on which is fixed, so to speak, the community gaze, and in our case it was on Arthur Wellses'. It was a curious, not unfriendly staring, much I dare say like that of the old robin who sees two young wild canaries building near her.

We passed the house, and went on to Mrs. Dane's.

She had given us no inkling of what we were to have that night, and my wife conjectured a conjurer! She gave me rather a triumphant smile when we were received in the library and the doors into the drawing-room were seen to be tightly closed.

We were early, as my wife is a punctual person, and soon after our arrival Sperry came. Mrs. Dane was in her chair as usual, with her companion in attendance, and when she heard Sperry's voice outside she excused herself and was wheeled out to him, and together we heard them go into the drawing-room. When the Robinsons arrived she and Sperry reappeared, and we waited for her customary announcement of the evening's program. When none came, even during the meal, I confess that my curiosity was almost painful.

I think, looking back, that it was Sperry who turned the talk to the supernatural, and that, to the accompaniment of considerable gibing by the men, he told a ghost story that set the women to looking back over their shoulders into the dark corners beyond the zone of candlelight. All of us, I remember, except Sperry and Mrs. Dane, were skeptical as to the supernatural, and Herbert Robinson believed that while there were so-called sensitives who actually went into trance, the controls which took possession of them were buried personalities of their own, released during trance from the sub-conscious mind.

"If not," he said truculently, "if they are really spirits, why can't they tell us what is going on, not in some vague place where they are always happy, but here and now, in the next house? I don't ask for prophecy, but for some evidence of their knowledge. For example, is Horace here the gay dog some of us suspect?"

As I am the Horace in question, I must explain that Herbert was merely being facetious. My life is a most orderly and decorous one. But my wife, unfortunately, lacks a sense of humor, and I felt that the remark might have been more fortunate.

"Physical phenomena!" scoffed the cynic. "I've seen it all—objects moving without visible hands, unexplained currents of cold air, voice through a trumpet—I know the whole rotten mess, and I've got a book which tells how to do all the tricks. I'll bring it along some night."

Mrs. Dane smiled, and the discussion was dropped for a time. It was during the coffee and cigars that Mrs. Dane made her announcement. As Alice Robinson takes an after-dinner cigarette, the ladies had remained with us at the table.

"As a matter of fact, Herbert," she said, "we intend to put your skepticism to the test tonight. Doctor Sperry has found a medium for us, a non-professional and a patient of his, and she has kindly consented to give us a sitting."

Herbert wheeled and looked at Sperry.

"Hold up your right hand and state by your honor as a member in good standing that you have not primed her, Sperry."

Sperry held up his hand.

"Absolutely not," he said, gravely. "She is coming in my car. She doesn't know to what house or whose. She knows none of you. She is a stranger to the city, and she will not even recognize the neighborhood."

Chapter 2

The butler wheeled out Mrs. Dane's chair, as her companion did not dine with her on club nights, and led us to the drawing-room doors. There Sperry threw them open, and we saw that the room had been completely metamorphosed.

Mrs. Dane's drawing-room is generally rather painful. Kindly soul that she is, she has considered it necessary to preserve and exhibit there the many gifts of a long lifetime. Photographs long outgrown, onyx tables, a clutter of odd chairs and groups of discordant bric-a-brac usually make the progress of her chair through it a precarious and perilous matter. We paused in the doorway, startled.

The room had been dismantled. It opened before us, walls and chimney-piece bare, rugs gone from the floor, even curtains taken from the windows. To emphasize the change, in the center stood a common pine table, surrounded by seven plain chairs. All the lights were out save one, a corner bracket, which was screened with a red-paper shade.

She watched our faces with keen satisfaction. "Such a time I had doing it!" she said. "The servants, of course, think I have gone mad. All except Clara. I told her. She's a sensible girl."

Herbert chuckled.

"Very neat," he said, "although a chair or two for the spooks would have been no more than hospitable. All right. Now bring on your ghosts."

My wife, however, looked slightly displeased. "As a church-woman," she said, "I really feel that it is positively impious to bring back the souls of the departed, before they are called from on High."

"Oh, rats," Herbert broke in rudely. "They'll not come. Don't worry. And if you hear raps, don't worry. It will probably be the medium cracking the joint of her big toe."

There was still a half hour until the medium's arrival. At Mrs. Dane's direction we employed it in searching the room. It was the ordinary rectangular drawing-room, occupying a corner of the house. Two windows at the end faced on the street, with a patch of railed-in lawn beneath them. A fireplace with a dying fire and flanked by two other windows, occupied the long side opposite the door into the hall. These windows, opening on a garden, were closed by outside shutters, now bolted. The third side was a blank wall, beyond which lay the library. On the fourth side were the double doors into the hall.

As, although the results we obtained were far beyond any expectations, the purely physical phenomena were relatively insignificant, it is not necessary to go further into the detail of the room. Robinson has done that, anyhow, for the Society of

Psychical Research, a proceeding to which I was opposed, as will be understood by the close of the narrative.

Further to satisfy Mrs. Dane, we examined the walls and floor-boards carefully, and Herbert, armed with a candle, went down to the cellar and investigated from below, returning to announce in a loud voice which made us all jump that it seemed all clear enough down there. After that we sat and waited; and I dare say the bareness and darkness of the room put us into excellent receptive condition. I know that I myself, probably owing to an astigmatism, once or twice felt that I saw wavering shadows in corners, and I felt again some of the strangeness I had felt during the day. We spoke in whispers, and Alice Robinson recited the history of a haunted house where she had visited in England. But Herbert was still cynical. He said, I remember:

"Here we are, six intelligent persons of above the average grade, and in a few minutes our hair will be rising and our pulses hammering while a Choctaw Indian control, in atrocious English, will tell us she is happy and we are happy and so everybody's happy. Hanky panky!"

"You may be as skeptical as you please, if you will only be fair, Herbert," Mrs. Dane said.

"And by that you mean—"

"During the sitting keep an open mind and a closed mouth," she replied cheerfully.

As I said at the beginning, this is not a ghost story. Parts of it we now understand, other parts we do not. For the physical phenomena we have no adequate explanation. They occurred. We saw and heard them. For the other part of the seance we have come to a conclusion satisfactory to ourselves, a conclusion not reached, however, until some of us had gone through some dangerous experiences, and had been brought into contact with things hitherto outside the orderly progression of our lives.

But at no time, although incredible things happened, did any one of us glimpse that strange world of the spirit that seemed so often almost within our range of vision.

Miss Jeremy, the medium, was due at 8:30 and at 8:20 my wife assisted Mrs. Dane into one of the straight chairs at the table, and Sperry, sent out by her, returned with a darkish bundle in his arms, and carrying a light bamboo rod.

"Don't ask me what they are for," he said to Herbert's grin of amusement. "Every workman has his tools."

Herbert examined the rod, but it was what it appeared to be, and nothing else.

Someone had started the phonograph in the library, and it was playing gloomily. At Sperry's request we stopped talking and composed ourselves, and Herbert, I remember, took a tablet of some sort, to our intense annoyance, and crunched it in his teeth. Then Miss Jeremy came in.

She was not at all what we had expected. Twenty-six, I should say, and in a black dinner dress. She seemed like a perfectly normal young woman, even attractive in a fragile, delicate way. Not much personality, perhaps; the very word "medium" precludes that. A "sensitive," I think she called herself. We were presented to her, and but for the stripped and bare room, it might have been any evening after any dinner, with bridge waiting.

When she shook hands with me she looked at me keenly. "What a strange day it has been!" she said. "I have been very nervous. I only hope I can do what you want this evening."

"I am not at all sure what we *do* want, Miss Jeremy," I replied.

She smiled a quick smile that was not without humor. Somehow I had never thought of a medium with a sense of humor. I liked her at once. We all liked her, and Sperry, Sperry the bachelor, the iconoclast, the antifeminist, was staring at her with curiously intent eyes.

Following her entrance Herbert had closed and bolted the drawing-room doors, and as an added precaution he now drew Mrs. Dane's empty wheeled chair across them.

"Anything that comes in," he boasted, "will come through the keyhole or down the chimney." And then, eying the fireplace, he deliberately took a picture from the wall and set it on the fender.

Miss Jeremy gave the room only the most casual of glances.

"Where shall I sit?" she asked.

Mrs. Dane indicated her place, and she asked for a small stand to be brought in and placed about two feet behind her chair, and two chairs to flank it, and then to take the black cloth from the table and hang it over the bamboo rod, which was laid across the backs of the chairs. Thus arranged, the curtain formed a low screen behind her, with the stand beyond it. On this stand we placed, at her order, various articles

131

from our pockets—I a fountain pen, Sperry a knife; and my wife contributed a gold bracelet.

We all felt, I fancy, rather absurd. Herbert's smile in the dim light became a grin. "The same old thing!" he whispered to me. "Watch her closely. They do it with a folding rod."

We arranged between us that we were to sit one on each side of her, and Sperry warned me not to let go of her hand for a moment. "They have a way of switching hands," he explained in a whisper. "If she wants to scratch her nose I'll scratch it."

We were, we discovered, not to touch the table, but to sit around it at a distance of a few inches, holding hands and thus forming the circle. And for twenty minutes we sat thus, and nothing happened. She was fully conscious and even spoke once or twice, and at last she moved impatiently and told us to put our hands on the table.

I had put my opened watch on the table before me, a night watch with a luminous dial. At five minutes after nine I felt the top of the table waver under my fingers, a curious, fluid-like motion.

"The table is going to move," I said.

Herbert laughed, a dry little chuckle. "Sure it is," he said. "When we all get to acting together, it will probably do considerable moving. I feel what you feel. It's flowing under my fingers."

"Blood," said Sperry. "You fellows feel the blood moving through the ends of your fingers. That's all. Don't be impatient."

However, curiously enough, the table did not move. Instead, my watch, before my eyes, slid to the edge of the table and dropped to the floor, and almost instantly an object, which we recognized later as Sperry's knife, was flung over the curtain and struck the wall behind Mrs. Dane violently.

One of the women screamed, ending in a hysterical giggle. Then we heard rhythmic beating on the top of the stand behind the medium. Startling as it was at the beginning, increasing as it did from a slow beat to an incredibly rapid drumming, when the initial shock was over Herbert commenced to gibe.

"Your fountain pen, Horace," he said to me. "Making out a statement for services rendered, by its eagerness."

The answer to that was the pen itself, aimed at him with apparent accuracy, and followed by an outcry from him.

"Here, stop it!" he said. "I've got ink all over me!"

We laughed consumedly. The sitting had taken on all the attributes of practical joking. The table no longer quivered under my hands.

"Please be sure you are holding my hands tight. Hold them very tight," said Miss Jeremy. Her voice sounded faint and far away. Her head was dropped forward on her chest, and she suddenly sagged in her chair. Sperry broke the circle and coming to her, took her pulse. It was, he reported, very rapid.

"You can move and talk now if you like," he said. "She's in trance, and there will be no more physical demonstrations."

Mrs. Dane was the first to speak. I was looking for my fountain pen, and Herbert was again examining the stand.

"I believe it now," Mrs. Dane said. "I saw your watch go, Horace, but tomorrow I won't believe it at all."

"How about your companion?" I asked. "Can she take shorthand? We ought to have a record."

"Probably not in the dark."

"We can have some light now," Sperry said.

There was a sort of restrained movement in the room now. Herbert turned on a bracket light, and I moved away the roller chair.

"Go and get Clara, Horace," Mrs. Dane said to me, "and have her bring a note-book and pencil." Nothing, I believe, happened during my absence. Miss Jeremy was sunk in her chair and breathing heavily when I came back with Clara, and Sperry was still watching her pulse. Suddenly my wife said:

"Why, look! She's wearing my bracelet!"

This proved to be the case, and was, I regret to say, the cause of a most unjust suspicion on my wife's part. Even today, with all the knowledge she possesses, I am certain that Mrs. Johnson believes that some mysterious power took my watch and dragged it off the table, and threw the pen, but that I myself under cover of darkness placed her bracelet on Miss Jeremy's arm. I can only reiterate here what I have told her many times, that I never touched the bracelet after it was placed on the stand.

"Take down everything that happens, Clara, and all we say," Mrs. Dane said in a low tone. "Even if it sounds like nonsense, put it down."

It is because Clara took her orders literally that I am making this more readable version of her script. There was a certain amount of non-pertinent matter which would only cloud the statement if rendered word for word, and also certain scattered, unrelated words with which many of the statements terminated. For instance, at the end of the sentence, "Just above the ear," came a number of rhymes to the final word, "dear, near, fear, cheer, three cheers." These I have cut, for the sake of clearness.

For some five minutes, perhaps, Miss Jeremy breathed stertorously, and it was during that interval that we introduced Clara and took up our positions. Sperry sat near the medium now, having changed places with Herbert, and the rest of us were as we had been, save that we no longer touched hands. Suddenly Miss Jeremy began to breathe more quietly, and to move about in her chair. Then she sat upright.

"Good evening, friends," she said. "I am glad to see you all again."

I caught Herbert's eye, and he grinned.

"Good evening, little Bright Eyes," he said. "How's everything in the happy hunting ground tonight?"

"Dark and cold," she said. "Dark and cold. And the knee hurts. It's very bad. If the key is on the nail— Arnica will take the pain out."

She lapsed into silence. In transcribing Clara's record I shall make no reference to these pauses, which were frequent, and occasionally filled in with extraneous matter. For instance, once there was what amounted to five minutes of Mother Goose jingles. Our method was simply one of question, by one of ourselves, and of answer by Miss Jeremy. These replies were usually in a querulous tone, and were often apparently unwilling. Also occasionally there was a bit of vernacular, as in the next reply. Herbert, who was still flippantly amused, said:

"Don't bother about your knee. Give us some local stuff. Gossip. If you can."

"Sure I can, and it will make your hair curl." Then suddenly there was a sort of dramatic pause and then an outburst.

"He's dead."

"Who is dead?" Sperry asked, with his voice drawn a trifle thin.

"A bullet just above the ear. That's a bad place. Thank goodness there's not much blood. Cool water will take it out of the carpet. Not hot. *Not hot.* Do you want to set the stain?"

"Look here," Sperry said, looking around the table. "I don't like this. It's darned grisly."

"Oh, fudge!" Herbert put in irreverently. "Let her rave, or it; or whatever it is. Do you mean that a man is dead?"—to the medium.

"Yes. She has the revolver. She needn't cry so. He was cruel to her. He was a beast. Sullen."

"Can you see the woman?" I asked.

"If it's sent out to be cleaned it will cause trouble. Hang it in the closet."

Herbert muttered something about the movies having nothing on us, and was angrily hushed. There was something quite outside of Miss Jeremy's words that had impressed itself on all of us with a sense of unexpected but very real tragedy. As I look back I believe it was a sort of desperation in her voice. But then came one of those interruptions which were to annoy us considerable during the series of sittings; she began to recite Childe Harold.

When that was over, "Now then," Sperry said in a

136

businesslike voice, "you see a dead man, and a young woman with him. Can you describe the room?"

"A small room, his dressing-room. He was shaving. There is still lather on his face."

"And the woman killed him?"

"I don't know. Oh, I don't know. No, she didn't. He did it!"

"He did it himself?"

There was no answer to that, but a sort of sulky silence.

"Are you getting this, Clara?" Mrs. Dane asked sharply. "Don't miss a word. Who knows what this may develop into?"

I looked at the secretary, and it was clear that she was terrified. I got up and took my chair to her. Coming back, I picked up my forgotten watch from the floor. It was still going, and the hands marked nine-thirty.

"Now," Sperry said in a soothing tone, "you said there was a shot fired and a man was killed. Where was this? What house?"

"Two shots. One is in the ceiling of the dressing-room."

"And the other killed him?"

But here, instead of a reply we got the words, "library paste."

Quite without warning the medium groaned, and Sperry believed the trance was over.

"She's coming out," he said. "A glass of wine, somebody." But she did not come out. Instead, she twisted in the chair.

"He's so heavy to lift," she muttered. Then: "Get the lather off his face. The lather. The lather."

137

She subsided into the chair and began to breathe with difficulty. "I want to go out. I want air. If I could only go to sleep and forget it. The drawing-room furniture is scattered over the house."

This last sentence she repeated over and over. It got on our nerves, ragged already.

"Can you tell us about the house?"

There was a distinct pause. Then: "Certainly. A brick house. The servants' entrance is locked, but the key is on a nail, among the vines. All the drawing-room furniture is scattered through the house."

"She must mean the furniture of this room," Mrs. Dane whispered.

The remainder of the sitting was chaotic. The secretary's notes consisted of unrelated words and often childish verses. On going over the notes the next day, when the stenographic record had been copied on a typewriter, Sperry and I found that one word recurred frequently. The word was "curtain."

Of the extraordinary event that followed the breaking up of the seance, I have the keenest recollection. Miss Jeremy came out of her trance weak and looking extremely ill, and Sperry's motor took her home. She knew nothing of what had happened, and hoped we had been satisfied. By agreement, we did not tell her what had transpired, and she was not curious.

Herbert saw her to the car, and came back, looking grave. We were standing together in the center of the dismantled room, with the lights going full now.

"Well," he said, "it is one of two things. Either we've been gloriously faked, or we've been let in on a very tidy little crime."

It was Mrs. Dane's custom to serve a Southern eggnog as a sort of stirr-up-cup—nightcap, she calls it—on her evenings, and we found it waiting for us in the library. In the warmth of its open fire, and the cheer of its lamps, even in the dignity and impassiveness of the butler, there was something sane and wholesome. The women of the party reacted quickly, but I looked over to see Sperry at a corner desk, intently working over a small object in the palm of his hand.

He started when he heard me, then laughed and held out his hand.

"Library paste!" he said. "It rolls into a soft, malleable ball, It could quite easily be used to fill a small hole in plaster. The paper would paste down over it too."

"Then you think—?"

"I'm not thinking at all. The thing she described may have taken place in Timbuctoo. May have happened ten years ago. May be the plot of some book she has read."

"On the other hand," I replied, "it is just possible that it was here, in this neighborhood, while we were sitting in that room."

"Have you any idea of the time?"

"I know exactly. It was half-past nine."

Chapter 3

At midnight, shortly after we reached home, Sperry called me on the phone. "Be careful, Horace," he said. "Don't let Mrs. Horace think anything has happened. I want to see you at once. Suppose you say I have a patient in a bad way, and a will to be drawn."

I listened to sounds from upstairs. I heard my wife go into her room and close the door.

"Tell me something about it," I urged.

"Just this. Arthur Wells killed himself tonight, shot himself in the head. I want you to go there with me."

"Arthur Wells!"

"Yes. I say, Horace, did you happen to notice the time the seance began tonight?"

"It was five minutes after nine when my watch fell."

"Then it would have been about half past when the trance began?"

"Yes."

There was a silence at Sperry's end of the wire.

Then: "He was shot about 9:30," he said, and rang off.

I am not ashamed to confess that my hands shook as I hung up the receiver. A brick house, she had said; the Wells house was brick. And so were all the other houses on the street. Vines in back? Well, even my own house had vines. It was absurd; it was pure coincidence; it was—well, I felt it was queer.

Nevertheless, as I stood there, I wondered for the first time in a highly material existence, whether there might not be, after all, a spirit-world surrounding us, cognizant of all that we did, touching but intangible, sentient but turned above our common senses?

I stood by the prosaic telephone instrument and looked into the darkened recesses of the passage. It seemed to my disordered nerves that back of the coats and wraps that hung on the rack, beyond the heavy curtains, in every corner, there lurked vague and shadowy forms, invisible when I stared, but advancing a trifle from their obscurity when, by turning my head and looking ahead, they impinged on the extreme right or left of my field of vision.

I was shocked by the news, but not greatly grieved. The Wellses had been among us but not of us, as I have said. They had come, like gay young comets, into our orderly constellation, trailing behind them their cars and servants, their children and governesses and rather riotous friends, and had flashed on us a sort of bright impermanence.

Of the two, I myself had preferred Arthur. His faults were on the surface. He drank hard, gambled, and could not always pay his gambling debts. But underneath it all there had always been something boyishly honest about him. He had played, it is true, through most of the thirty years that now marked his whole life, but he could have been made a man by the right woman. And he had married the wrong one.

Of Elinor Wells I have only my wife's verdict, and I have found that, as is the way with many good women, her judgments of her own sex are rather merciless. A tall, handsome girl, very dark, my wife has characterized her as cold, calculating and ambitious. She has said frequently, too, that Elinor Wells was a disappointed woman, that her marriage, while giving her social identity, had disappointed her in a monetary way. Whether that is true or not, there was no doubt, by the time they had lived in our neighborhood for a year, that a complication had arisen in the shape of another man.

My wife, on my return from my office in the evening, had been quite likely to greet me with:

"Horace, he has been there all afternoon. I really think something should be done about it."

"Who has been where?" I would ask, not too patiently.

"You know perfectly well. And I think you ought to tell him."

In spite of her vague pronouns, I understood, and in a more masculine way I shared her sense of outrage. Our street has never had a scandal on it, except the one when the Berringtons' music teacher ran away with their coachman, in the days of carriages. And I am glad to say that that is almost forgotten.

Nevertheless, we had realized for some time that

the dreaded triangle was threatening the repute of our quiet neighborhood, and as I stood by the telephone that night I saw that it had come. More than that, it seemed very probable that into this very triangle our peaceful Neighborhood Club had been suddenly thrust.

My wife accepted my excuse coldly. She dislikes intensely the occasional outside calls of my profession. She merely observed, however, that she would leave all the lights on until my return. "I should think you could arrange things better, Horace," she added. "It's perfectly idiotic the way people die at night. And tonight, of all nights!"

I shall have to confess that through all of the thirty years of our married life my wife has clung to the belief that I am a bit of a dog. Thirty years of exemplary living have not affected this conviction, nor had Herbert's foolish remark earlier in the evening helped matters. But she watched me put on my overcoat without further comment. When I kissed her good-night, however, she turned her cheek.

The street, with its open spaces, was a relief after the dark hall. I started for Sperry's house, my head bent against the wind, my mind on the news I had just heard. Was it, I wondered, just possible that we had for some reason been allowed behind the veil which covered poor Wells's last moments? And, to admit that for a moment, where would what we had heard lead us? Sperry had said he had killed himself. But—suppose he had not?

I realize now, looking back, that my recollection of the other man in the triangle is largely colored by the

143

fact that he was killed in the war. At that time I hardly knew him, except as a wealthy and self-made man in his late thirties; I saw him now and then, in the club playing billiards or going in and out of the Wells house, a large, fastidiously dressed man, strong featured and broad shouldered, with rather too much manner.

A man who would go straight for the thing he wanted, woman or power or money. And get it.

Sperry was waiting on his doorstep, and we went on to the Wells house. What with the magnitude of the thing that had happened, and our mutual feeling that we were somehow involved in it, we were rather silent. Sperry asked one question, however, "Are you certain about the time when Miss Jeremy saw what looks like this thing?"

"Certainly. My watch fell at five minutes after nine. When it was all over, and I picked it up, it was still going, and it was 9:30."

He was silent for a moment. Then:

"The Wellses' nursery governess telephoned for me at 9:35. We keep a record of the time of all calls."

Sperry is a heart specialist, I think I have said, with offices in his house.

And, a block or so farther on: "I suppose it was bound to come. To tell the truth, I didn't think the boy had the courage."

"Then you think he did it?"

"They say so," he said grimly. And added, irritably: "Good heavens, Horace, we must keep that other fool thing out of our minds."

"Yes," I agreed. "We must."

Although the Wells house was brilliantly lighted

144

when we reached it, we had difficulty in gaining admission. Whoever were in the house were upstairs, and the bell evidently rang in the deserted kitchen or a neighboring pantry.

"We might try the servants' entrance," Sperry said. Then he laughed mirthlessly.

"We might see," he said, "if there's a key on the nail among the vines."

I confess to a nervous tightening of my muscles as we made our way around the house. If the key was there, we were on the track of a revelation that might revolutionize much that we had held fundamental in science and in our knowledge of life itself. If, sitting in Mrs. Dane's quiet room, a woman could tell us what was happening in a house a mile or so away, it opened up a new earth. Almost a new heaven.

I stopped and touched Sperry's arm. "This Miss Jeremy—did she know Arthur Wells or Elinor? If she knew the house, and the situation between them, isn't it barely possible that she anticipated this thing?"

"We knew them," he said gruffly, "and whatever we anticipated, it wasn't this."

Sperry had a pocket flash, and when we found the door locked we proceeded with our search for the key. The porch had been covered with heavy vines, now dead of the November frosts, and showing, here and there, dead and dried leaves that crackled as we touched them. In the darkness something leaped against me, and I almost cried out. It was, however, only a collie dog, eager for the warmth of his place by the kitchen fire.

"Here's the key," Sperry said, and held it out. The

flash wavered in his hand, and his voice was strained.

"So far, so good," I replied, and was conscious that my own voice rang strange in my ears.

We admitted ourselves, and the dog, bounding past us, gave a sharp yelp of gratitude and ran into the kitchen.

"Look here, Sperry," I said, as we stood inside the door, "they don't want me here. They've sent for you, but I'm the most casual sort of an acquaintance. I haven't any business here."

That struck him, too. We had both been so obsessed with the scene at Mrs. Dane's that we had not thought of anything else.

"Suppose you sit down in the library," he said. "The chances are against her coming down, and the servants don't matter."

As a matter of fact, we learned later that all the servants were out except the nursery governess. There were two small children. There was a servants' ball somewhere and, with the exception of the butler, it was after two before they commenced to straggle in. Except two plain-clothes men from the central office, a physician who was with Elinor in her room, and the governess, there was no one else in the house but the children, asleep in the nursery.

As I sat alone in the library, the house was perfectly silent. But in some strange fashion it had apparently taken on the attributes of the deed that had preceded the silence. It was sinister, mysterious, dark. Its immediate effect on my imagination was apprehension—almost terror. Murder or suicide, here among the shadows a soul, an indestructible thing, had been recently violently wrenched from its body. The body lay in the room overhead. But what of the spirit? I shivered as I thought that it might even then be watching me with formless eyes from some dark corner.

Overwrought as I was, I was forced to bring my common sense to bear on the situation. Here was a tragedy, a real and terrible one. Suppose we had, in some queer fashion, touched its outer edges that night? Then how was it that there had come, mixed up with so much that might be pertinent, such extraneous and grosteque things as Childe Harold, a hurt knee, and Mother Goose?

I remember moving impatiently, and trying to argue myself into my ordinary logical state of mind, but I know now that even then I was wondering whether Sperry had found a hole in the ceiling upstairs.

I wandered, I recall, into the realm of the clairvoyant and the clairaudient. Under certain conditions, such as trance, I knew that some individuals claimed a power of vision that was supernormal, and I had at one time lunched at my club with a well-dressed gentleman in a *pince nez* who said the room was full of people I could not see, but who were perfectly distinct to him. He claimed, and I certainly could not refute him, that he saw further into the violet of the spectrum than the rest of us, and seemed to consider it nothing unusual when an elderly woman, whose description sounded much like my great-grandmother, came and stood behind my chair.

I recall that he said she was stroking my hair, and that following that I had a distinctly creepy sensation along my scalp.

Then there were those who claimed that in trance the spirit of the medium, giving place to a control, was free to roam whither it would, and, although I am not sure of this that it wandered in the fourth dimension. While I am very vague about the fourth dimension, I did know that in it doors and walls were not obstacles. But as they would not be obstacles to a spirit, even in the world as we know it, that got me nowhere.

Suppose Sperry came down and said Arthur Wells had been shot above the ear, and that there was a second bullet hole in the ceiling? Added to the key on the nail, a careless custom and surely not common, we would have conclusive proof that our medium had been correct. There was another point, too. Miss Jeremy had said, "Get the lather off his face."

That brought me up with a turn. Would a man stop shaving to kill himself? If he did, why a revolver? Why not the razor in his hand?

I knew from my law experience that suicide is either a desperate impulse or a cold-blooded and calculated finality. A man who kills himself while dressing comes under the former classification, and will usually seize the first method at hand. But there was something else, too. Shaving is an automatic process. It completes itself. My wife has an irritated conviction that if the house caught fire while I was in the midst of the process, I would complete it and rinse the soap from my face before I caught up the fire-extinguisher.

Had he killed himself, or had Elinor killed him? Was she the sort of sacrifice herself to a violent impulse? Would she choose the hard way, when there was the easy one of the divorce court? I thought not. And the same was true of Ellingham. Here were two people, both of them careful of appearance, if not of fact. There was another possibility, too. That he had learned something while he was dressing, had attacked or threatened her with a razor, and she had killed him in self-defense.

I had reached that point when Sperry came down the staircase, ushering out the detectives and the medical man. He came to the library door and stood looking at me, with his face rather paler than usual.

"I'll take you up now," he said. "She's in her room, in bed, and she has had an opiate."

"Was he shot above the ear?"

"Yes."

I did not look at him, nor he at me. We climbed the stairs and entered the room, where, according to Elinor's story, Arthur Wells had killed himself. It was a dressing-room, as Miss Jeremy had described. A wardrobe, a table with books and magazines in disorder, two chairs, and a couch, constituted the furnishings. Beyond was a bathroom. On a chair by a window the dead man's evening clothes were neatly laid out, his shoes beneath. His top hat and folded gloves were on the table.

Arthur Wells lay on the couch. A sheet had been drawn over the body, and I did not disturb it. It gave the impression of unusual length that is always found, I think, in the dead, and a breath of air from an open window, by stirring the sheet, gave a false appearance of life beneath.

The house was absolutely still.

When I glanced at Sperry he was staring at the ceiling, and I followed his eyes, but there was no mark on it. Sperry made a little gesture.

"It's queer," he muttered. "It's—"

"The detective and I put him there. He was here." He showed a place on the floor midway of the room.

"Where was his head lying?" I asked, cautiously.

"Here."

I stooped and examined the carpet. It was a dark Oriental, with much red in it. I touched the place, and then ran my folded handkerchief over it. It came up stained with blood.

"There would be no object in using cold water there, so as not to set the stain," Sperry said thoughtfully. "Whether he fell there or not, that is where she allowed him to be found."

"You don't think he fell there?"

"She dragged him, didn't she?" he demanded. Then the strangeness of what he was saying struck him, and he smiled foolishly. "What I mean is, the medium said she did. I don't suppose any jury would pass us tonight as entirely sane, Horace," he said.

He walked across to the bathroom and surveyed it from the doorway. I followed him. It was as orderly as the other room. On a glass shelf over the washstand was his razor, a safety and, beside it, in a black case, an assortment of the long-bladed variety.

Sperry stood thoughtfully in the doorway.

"The servants are out," he said. "According to Elinor's statement he was dressing when he did it. And yet someone has had a wild impulse for tidiness here, since it happened. Not a towel out of place!"

It was in the bathroom that he told me Elinor's

story. According to her, it was a simple case of suicide. And she was honest about it, in her own way. She was shocked, but she was not pretending any wild grief. She hadn't wanted him to die, but she had not felt that they could go on much longer together. There had been no quarrel other than their usual bickering. They had been going to a dance that night. The servants had all gone out immediately after dinner to a servants' ball and the governess had gone for a walk. She was to return at nine-thirty to fasten Elinor's gown and to be with the children.

Arthur, she said, had been depressed for several days, and at dinner had hardly spoken at all. He had not, however, objected to the dance. He had, indeed, seemed strangely determined to go, although she had pleaded a headache. At nine o'clock he went upstairs, apparently to dress.

She was in her room, with the door shut, when she heard a shot. She ran in and found him lying on the floor of his dressing-room with his revolver behind him. The governess was still out. The shot had roused the children, and they had come down from the nursery above. She was frantic, but she had to soothe them. The governess, however, came in almost immediately, and she had sent her to the telephone to summon help, calling Sperry first of all, and then the police.

"Have you seen the revolver?" I asked.

"Yes. It's all right, apparently. Only one shot had been fired."

"How soon did they get a doctor?"

"It must have been some time. They gave up telephoning, and the governess went out, finally, and found one."

"Then, while she was out—?"

"Possibly," Sperry said. "If we start with the hypothesis that she is lying."

"If she cleaned up here for any reason," I began, and commenced a desultory examination of the room. Just why I looked behind the bathtub forces me to an explanation I am somewhat loath to make, but which will explain a rather unusual proceeding. For some time my wife has felt that I smoked too heavily, and out of her solicitude for me has limited me to one cigar after dinner. But as I have been a heavy smoker for years I have found this a great hardship, and have therefore kept a reserve store, by arrangement with the housemaid, behind my tub. In self-defense I must also state that I seldom have recourse to such stealthy measures.

Believing then that something might possibly be hidden there, I made an investigation, and could see some small objects lying there. Sperry brought me a stick from the dressing-room, and with its aid I succeeded in bringing out the two articles which were instrumental in starting us on our brief but adventurous careers as private investigators. One was a leather razorstrop, old and stiff from disuse, and the other a wet bath sponge, now stained with blood to a yellowish brown.

"She is lying, Sperry," I said. "He fell somewhere else, and she dragged him to where he was found."

"But—why?"

"I don't know," I said impatiently. "From some place where a man would be unlikely to kill himself, I dare say. No one ever killed himself, for instance, in an open hallway. Or stopped shaving to do it."

"We have only Miss Jeremy's word for that," he said sullenly. "Confound it, Horace, don't let's bring in that stuff if we can help it."

We stared at each other, with the strop and the sponge between us. Suddenly he turned on his heel and went back into the room, and a moment later he called me, quietly.

"You're right," he said. "The poor devil was shaving. He had it half done. Come and look."

But I did not go. There was a carafe of water in the bathroom, I took a drink from it. My hands were shaking. When I turned around I found Sperry in the hall, examining the carpet with his flash light, and now and then stooping to run his hand over the floor.

"Nothing here," he said in a low tone, when I had joined him. "At least I haven't found anything."

Chapter 4

How much of Sperry's proceeding with the carpet the governess had seen I do not know. I glanced up and she was there, on the staircase to the third floor, watching us. I did not know, then, whether she recognized me or not, for the Wellses' servants were as oblivious of the families on the street as their employers. But she knew Sperry, and was ready enough to talk to him.

"How is she now?" she asked.

"She is sleeping, Mademoiselle."

"The children also."

She came down the stairs, a lean young Frenchwoman in a dark dressing gown, and Sperry suggested that she too should have an opiate. She seized at the idea, but Sperry did not go down at once for his professional bag.

"You were not here when it occurred, Mademoiselle?" he inquired.

"No, doctor. I had been out for a walk." She clasped her hands. "When I came back—"

"Was he still on the floor of the dressing-room when you came in?"

"But yes. Of course. She was alone. She could not lift him."

"I see," Sperry said thoughtfully. "No, I dare say she couldn't. Was the revolver on the floor also?"

"Yes, doctor. I myself picked it up."

To Sperry she showed, I observed, a slight deference, but when she glanced at me, as she did after each reply, I thought her expression slightly altered. At the time this puzzled me, but it was explained when Sperry started down the stairs.

"Monsieur is of the police?" she asked, with a Frenchwoman's timid respect for the constabulary.

I hesitated before I answered. I am a truthful man, and I hate unnecessary lying. But I ask consideration of the circumstances. Neither then nor at any time later was the solving of the Wells mystery the prime motive behind the course I laid out and consistently followed. I felt that we might be on the verge of some great psychic discovery, one which would revolutionize human thought and to a certain extent human action. And toward that end I was prepared to go to almost any length.

"I am making a few investigations," I told her. "You say Mrs. Wells was alone in the house, except for her husband?"

"The children."

"Mr. Wells was shaving, I believe, when the—er— impulse overtook him?"

There was no doubt as to her surprise. "Shaving? I think not."

"What sort of razor did he ordinarily use?"

"A safety razor always. At least I have never seen any others around."

"There is a case of old-fashioned razors in the bathroom."

She glanced toward the room and shrugged her shoulders. "Possibly he used others. I have not seen any."

"It was you, I suppose, who cleaned up afterward."

"Cleaned up?"

"You who washed up the stains."

"Stains? Oh, no, monsieur. Nothing of the sort has yet been done."

I felt that she was telling the truth, so far as she knew it, and I then asked about the revolver.

"Do you know where Mr. Wells kept his revolver?"

"When I first came it was in the drawer of that table. I suggested that it be placed beyond the children's reach. I do not know where it was put."

"Do you recall how you left the front door when you went out? I mean, was it locked?"

"No. The servants were out, and I knew there would be no one to admit me. I left it unfastened."

But it was evident that she had broken a rule of the house by doing so, for she added: "I am afraid to use the servants' entrance. It is dark there."

"The key is always hung on the nail when they are out?"

"Yes. If any one of them is out it is left there. There is only one key. The family is out a great deal, and it saves bringing someone down from the servants' rooms at the top of the house."

But I think my knowledge of the key bothered her, for some reason. And as I read over my questions, certainly they indicated a suspicion that the situation was less simple than it appeared. She shot a quick glance at me.

"Did you examine the revolver when you picked it up?"

"I, monsieur? *Non!*" Then her fears, whatever they were, got the best of her. "I know nothing but what I tell you. I was out. I can prove that that is so. I went to a pharmacy; the clerk will remember. I will go with you, monsieur, and he will tell you that I used the telephone there."

I dare say my business of cross-examination, of watching evidence, helped me to my next question.

"You went out to telephone when there is a telephone in the house?"

But here again, as once or twice before, a veil dropped between us. She avoided my eyes. "There are things one does not want the family to hear," she muttered. Then, having determined on a course of action, she followed it. "I am looking for another position. I do not like it here. The children are spoiled. I only came for a month's trial.

"And the pharmacy?"

"Elliott's, at the corner of State Avenue and McKee Street."

I told her that it would not be necessary for her to go to the pharmacy, and she muttered something about the children and went up the stairs. When Sperry came back with the opiate she was nowhere in sight, and he was considerably annoyed.

"She knows something," I told him. "She is frightened."

Sperry eyed me with a half frown.

"Now see here, Horace," he said, "suppose we had come in here, without the thought of that seance behind us? We'd have accepted the thing as it appears to be, wouldn't we? There may be a dozen explanations for that sponge, and for the razor strop. What in heaven's name has a razor strop to do with it anyhow? One bullet was fired, and the revolver has one empty chamber. It may not be the custom to stop shaving in order to commit suicide, but that's no argument that it can't be done, and as to the key—how do I know that my own back door key isn't hung outside on a nail sometimes?"

"We might look again for that hole in the ceiling."

"I won't do it. Miss Jeremy has read of something of that sort, or heard of it, and stored it in her subconscious mind."

But he glanced up at the ceiling nevertheless, and a moment later had drawn up a chair and stepped onto it, and I did the same thing. We presented, I imagine, rather a strange picture, and I know that the presence or the rigid figure on the couch gave me a sort of ghoulish feeling.

The house was an old one, and in the center of the high ceiling a plaster ornament surrounded the chandelier. Our search gradually centered on this ornament, but the chairs were low and our long-distance examination revealed nothing. It was at that time, too, that we heard someone in the lower hall, and we had only a moment to put our chairs in place before the butler came in. He showed no surprise, but stood looking at the body on the couch, his thin face working.

"I met the detectives outside, doctor," he said. "It's

a terrible thing, sir, a terrible thing."

"I'd keep the other servants out of this room, Hawkins."

"Yes, sir." He went over to the sheet, lifted the edge slowly, and then replaced it, and tiptoed to the door. "The others are not back yet. I'll admit them, and get them up quietly. How is Mrs. Wells?"

"Sleeping," Sperry said briefly, and Hawkins went out.

I realize now that Sperry was—I am sure he will forgive this—in a state of nerves that night. For example, he returned only an impatient silence to my doubt as to whether Hawkins had really only just returned and he quite missed something downstairs which I later proved to have an important bearing on the case. This was when we were going out, and after Hawkins had opened the front door for us. It had been freezing hard, and Sperry, who has a bad ankle, looked about for a walking stick. He found one, and I saw Hawkins take a swift step forward, and then stop, with no expression whatever in his face.

"This will answer, Hawkins."

"Yes, sir," said Hawkins impassively.

And if I realize that Sperry was nervous that night, I also realize that he was fighting a battle quite his own, and with its personal problems.

"She's got to quit this sort of thing," he said savagely and apropos of nothing, as we walked along. "It's hard on her, and besides—"

"Yes?"

"She couldn't have learned about it," he said, following his own trail of thought. "My car brought her from her home to the house door. She was brought in to us at once. But don't you see that if there are other developments, to prove her statements, she—well, she's as innocent as a child, but take Herbert, for instance. Do you suppose he'll believe she had no outside information?"

"But it was happening while we were shut in the drawing-room."

"So Elinor claims. But if there was anything to hide, it would have taken time. An hour or so, perhaps. You can see how Herbert would jump on that."

We went back, I remember, to speaking of the seance itself, and to the safer subject of the physical phenomena. As I have said, we did not then know of those experimenters who claim that the medium can evoke so-called rods of energy, and that by its means the invisible "controls" can perform their strange feats of levitation and the movement of solid bodies. Sperry touched very lightly on the spirit side.

"At least it would mean activity," he said. "The thought of an inert eternity is not bearable."

He was inclined, however, to believe that there were laws of which we were still in ignorance, and that we might some day find and use the fourth dimension. He seemed to be able to grasp it quite clearly. "The cube of the cube, or hyper-cube," he explained. "Or get it this way: a cone passed apex-downward through a plane."

"I know," I said, "that it is perfectly simple. But somehow it just sounds like words to me."

"It's perfectly clear, Horace," he insisted. "But remember this when you try to work it out; it is necessary to use motion as a translator of time into space, or of space into time."

"I don't intend to work it out," I said irritably. "But I mean to use motion as a translator of the time, which is 1:30 in the morning, to take me to a certain space, which is where I live."

But as it happened, I did not go into my house when I reached it. I was wide awake, and I perceived, on looking up at my wife's windows, that the lights were out. As it is her custom to wait up for me on those rare occasions when I spend an evening away from home, I surmised that she was comfortably asleep, and made my way to the pharmacy to which the Wellses' governess had referred.

The night-clerk was in the prescription-room behind the shop. He had fixed himself comfortably on two chairs, with an old table-cover over his knee and a half-empty bottle of sarsaparilla on a wooden box beside him. He did not waken until I spoke to him.

"Sorry to rouse you, Jim," I said.

He flung off the cover and jumped up, upsetting the bottle, which trickled a stale stream to the floor. "Oh, that's all right, Mr. Johnson, I wasn't asleep anyhow."

I let that go, and went at once to the object of our visit. Yes, he remembered the governess, knew her, as a matter of fact. The Wellses bought a good many things there. Asked as to her telephoning, he thought it was about nine o'clock, maybe earlier. But questioned as to what she had telephoned about, he drew himself up.

"Oh, see here," he said. "I can't very well tell you that, can I? This business has got ethics, all sorts

161

of ethics."

He enlarged on that. The secrets of the city, he maintained loftily, were in the hands of the pharmacies. It was a trust that they kept. "Every trouble from dope to drink, and then some," he boasted.

When I told him that Arthur Wells was dead his jaw dropped, but there was no more argument in him. He knew very well the number the governess had called.

"She's done it several times," he said. "I'll be frank with you. I got curious after the third evening, and called it myself. You know the trick. I found out it was the Ellingham house, up State Street."

"What was the nature of the conversations?"

"Oh, she was very careful. It's an open phone and anyone could hear her. Once she said somebody was not to come. Another time she just said, 'This is Suzanne Gautier. 9:30, please.'"

"And tonight?"

"That the family was going out—not to call."

When I told him it was a case of suicide, his jaw dropped.

"Can you beat it?" he said. "I ask you, can you beat it? A fellow who had everything!"

But he was philosophical, too.

"A lot of people get the bug once in a while," he said. "They come in here for a dose of sudden death, and it takes watching. You'd be surprised the number of things that will do the trick if you take enough. I don't know. If things get to breaking wrong—"

His voice trailed off, and he kicked at the old tablecover on the floor.

"It's a matter of the point of view," he said more

162

cheerfully. "And my point of view just now is that this place is darned cold, and so's the street. You'd better have a little something to warm you up before you go out, Mr. Johnson."

I was chilled through, to tell the truth, and although I rarely drink anything I went back with him and took an ounce or two of villainous whisky, poured out of a jug into a graduated glass. It is with deep humiliation of spirit I record that a housemaid coming into my library at seven o'clock the next morning, found me, in hat and overcoat, asleep on the library couch.

I had, however, removed my collar and tie, and my watch, carefully wound, was on the smoking-stand beside me.

Chapter 5

The death of Arthur Wells had taken place on Monday evening. Tuesday brought nothing new. The coroner was apparently satisfied, and on Wednesday the dead man's body was cremated.

"Thus obliterating all evidence," Sperry said, with what I felt was a note of relief.

But I think the situation was bothering him, and that he hoped to discount in advance the second sitting by Miss Jeremy, which Mrs. Dane had already arranged for the following Monday, for on Wednesday afternoon, following a conversation over the telephone, Sperry and I had a private sitting with Miss Jeremy in Sperry's private office. I took my wife into our confidence and invited her to be present, but the unfortunate coldness following the housemaid's discovery of me asleep in the library on the morning after the murder, was still noticeable and she refused.

The sitting, however, was totally without value. There was difficulty on the medium's part in securing the trance condition, and she broke out once

164

rather petulantly, with the remark that we were interfering with her in some way.

I noticed that Sperry had placed Arthur Wells's walking-stick unobtrusively on his table, but we secured only rambling and non-pertinent replies to our questions, and whether it was because I knew that outside it was broad day, or because the Wells matter did not come up at all I found a total lack of that sense of the unknown which made all the evening sittings so grisly.

I am sure she knew we had wanted something, and that she had failed to give it to us, for when she came out she was depressed and in a state of lowered vitality.

"I'm afraid I'm not helping you," she said. "I'm a little tired, I think."

She was tired. I felt suddenly very sorry for her. She was so pretty and so young—only twenty-six or thereabouts—to be in the grip of forces so relentless. Sperry sent her home in his car, and took to pacing the floor of his office.

"I'm going to give it up, Horace," he said. "Perhaps you are right. We may be on the verge of some real discovery. But while I'm interested, so interested that it interferes with my work, I'm frankly afraid to go on. There are several reasons."

I argued with him. There could be no question that if things were left as they were, a number of people would go through life convinced that Elinor Wells had murdered her husband. Look at the situation. She had sent out all the servants and the governess, surely an unusual thing in an establishment of that sort. And Miss Jeremy had been vindicated in three points; some stains had certainly been washed up, we had found the key where she had stated it to be, and Arthur had certainly been shaving himself.

"In other words," I argued, "we can't stop, Sperry. You can't stop. But my idea would be that our investigations be purely scientific and not criminal."

"Also, in other words," he said, "you think we will discover something, so you suggest that we compound a felony and keep it to ourselves!"

"Exactly," I said drily. . . .

It is of course possible that my nerves were somewhat unstrung during the days that followed. I wakened one night to a terrific thump which shook my bed, and which seemed to be the result of someone having struck the foot-board with a plank. Immediately following this came a sharp knocking on the antique bed-warmer which hangs beside my fireplace. When I had sufficiently recovered my self-control I turned on my bedside lamp, but the room was empty.

Again I wakened with a feeling of intense cold. I was frozen with it, and curiously enough it was an inner cold. It seemed to have nothing to do with the surface of my body. I have no explanation to make of these phenomena. Like the occurrences at the seance, they were, and that was all.

But on Thursday night of that week my wife came into my bedroom, and stated flatly that there were burglars in the house.

Now it has been my contention always that if a burglar gains entrance, he should be allowed to take what he wants. Silver can be replaced, but as I said to my wife then, Horace Johnson could not. But she had recently acquired a tea set formerly belonging to her great-grandmother, and apprehension regarding it made her, for the nonce, less solicitous for me than usual.

"Either you go or I go," she said. "Where's your revolver?"

I got out of bed at that, and went down the stairs. But I must confess that I felt, the moment darkness surrounded me, considerably less trepidation concerning the possible burglar than I felt as to the darkness itself. Mrs. Johnson had locked herself in my bedroom, and there was something horrible in the black depths of the lower hall.

From some strange inner compulsion I did not turn on the electric light. I carried a box of matches, but at the foot of the stairs the one I had lighted went out. I was terrified. I tried to light another match, but there was a draft from somewhere, and it too was extinguished before I had had time to glance about. I was immediately conscious of a sort of soft movement around me, as of shadowy shapes that passed and repassed. Once it seemed to me that a hand was laid on my shoulder and was not lifted, but instead dissolved into the other shadows around. The sudden striking of the clock on the stair landing completed my demoralization. I turned and fled upstairs, pursued, to my agonized nerves, by ghostly hands that came toward me from between the spindles of the stair-rail.

At dawn I went downstairs again, heartily ashamed of myself. I found that a door to the basement had been left open, and that the soft movement had probably been my overcoat, swaying in the draft.

Probably. I was not certain. Indeed, I was certain of nothing during those strange days. I had built up for myself a universe upheld by certain laws, of day and night, of food and sleep and movement, of three dimensions of space. And now, it seemed to me, I had stood all my life but on the threshold, and, for an hour or so, the door had opened.

Sperry had, I believe, told Herbert Robinson of what we had discovered, but nothing had been said to the women. I knew through my wife that they were wildly curious, and the night of the second seance Mrs. Dane drew me aside and I saw that she suspected, without knowing, that we had been endeavoring to check up our revelations with the facts.

"I want you to promise me one thing," she said. "I'll not bother you now. But I'm an old woman, with not much more of life to be influenced by any disclosures. When this thing is over, and you have come to a conclusion—I'll not put it that way: you may not come to a conclusion—but when it is over, I want you to tell me the whole story. Will you?"

I promised that I would.

Miss Jeremy did not come to dinner. She never ate before a seance. And although we tried to keep the conversational ball floating airily, there was not the usual effervescence of the Neighborhood Club dinners. One and all, we were waiting, we knew not for what.

I am sorry to record that there were no physical phenomena of any sort at this second seance. The room was arranged as it had been at the first sitting, except that a table with a candle and a chair had been placed behind a screen for Mrs. Dane's secretary.

There was one other change. Sperry had brought the walking-stick he had taken from Arthur Wells's room, and after the medium was in trance he placed it on the table before her.

The first questions were disappointing in results. Asked about the stick, there was only silence. When, however, Sperry went back to the sitting of the week before, and referred to questions and answers at that time, the medium seemed uneasy. Her hand, held under mine, made an effort to free itself, and, released, touched the cane. She lifted it, and struck the table a hard blow with it.

"Do you know to whom that stick belongs?" A silence. Then: "Yes."

"Will you tell us what you know about it?"

"It is writing."

"Writing?"

"It was writing, but the water washed it away."

Then, instantly and with great rapidity, followed a wild torrent of words and incomplete sentences. It was inarticulate, and the secretary made no record of it. As I recall, however, it was about water, children, and the words "ten o'clock" repeated several times.

"Do you mean that something happened at ten o'clock?"

"No. Certainly not. No, indeed. The water washed it away. All of it, Not a trace."

"Where did all this happen?"

She named, without hesitation, a seaside resort about fifty miles from our city. There was not one of

169

us, I dare say, who did not know that the Wellses had spent the preceding summer there and that Charlie Ellingham had been there, also.

"Do you know that Arthur Wells is dead?"

"Yes. He is dead."

"Did he kill himself?"

"You can't catch me on that. I don't know."

Here the medium laughed. It was horrible. And the laughter made the whole thing absurd. But it died away quickly.

"If only the pocketbook was not lost," she said. "There were so many things in it. Especially car-tickets. Walking is a nuisance."

Mrs. Dane's secretary suddenly spoke. "Do you want me to take things like that?" she asked.

"Take everything, please," was the answer.

"Car-tickets and letters. It will be terrible if the letters are found."

"Where was the pocketbook lost?" Sperry asked.

"If that were known, it could be found," was the reply, rather sharply given. "Hawkins may have it. He was always hanging around. The curtain was much safer."

"What curtain?"

"Nobody would have thought of the curtain. First ideas are best."

She repeated this, following it, as once before, with rhymes for the final word, best, rest, chest, pest.

"Pest!" she said. "That's Hawkins!" And again the laughter.

"Did one of the bullets strike the ceiling?"

"Yes. But you'll never find it. It is holding well. That part's safe enough—unless it made a hole in the floor above."

"But there was only one empty chamber in the revolver. How could two shots have been fired?"

There was no answer at all to this. And Sperry, after waiting, went on to his next question: "Who occupied the room overhead?"

But here we received the reply to the previous question: "There was a box of cartridges in the table-drawer. That's easy."

From that point, however, the interest lapsed. Either there was no answer to questions, or we got the absurdity that we had encountered before, about the drawing-room furniture. But, unsatisfactory in many ways as the seance had been, the effect on Miss Jeremy was profound—she was longer in coming out, and greatly exhausted when it was all over.

She refused to take the supper Mrs. Dane had prepared for her, and at eleven o'clock Sperry took her home in his car.

I remember that Mrs. Dane inquired, after she had gone. "Does anyone know the name of the Wellses' butler? Is it Hawkins?"

I said nothing, and as Sperry was the only one likely to know and he had gone, the inquiry went no further. Looking back, I realize that Herbert, while less cynical, was still skeptical, that his sister was noncommittal, but for some reason watching me, and that Mrs. Dane was in a state of delightful anticipation.

My wife, however, had taken a dislike to Miss Jeremy, and said that the whole thing bored her.

"The men like it, of course," she said. "Horace fairly simpers with pleasure while he sits and holds

171

her hand. But a woman doesn't impose on other women so easily. It's silly."

"My dear," Mrs. Dane said, reaching over and patting my wife's hand, "people talked that way about Columbus and Galileo. And if it *is* nonsense, it is such thrilling nonsense!"

Chapter 6

I find that the solution of the Arthur Wells mystery—
for we did solve it—takes three divisions in my mind.
Each one is a sitting, followed by an investigation
made by Sperry and myself.

But for some reason, after Miss Jeremy's second
sitting, I found that my reasoning mind was stronger
than my credulity. And as Sperry had at that time
determined to have nothing more to do with the
business, I made a resolution to abandon my investigations. Nor have I any reason to believe that I
would have altered my attitude toward the case had it
not been that I saw in the morning paper, on the
Thursday following the second seance, that Elinor
Wells had closed her house and gone to Florida.

I tried to put the fact out of my mind that morning.
After all, what good would it do? No discovery of
mine could bring Arthur Wells back to his family, to
his seat at the bridge table at the club, to his too
expensive cars and his unpaid bills. Or to his wife
who was not grieving for him.

On the other hand, I confess to an overwhelming desire to examine again the ceiling of the dressing-room and thus to check up one degree further the accuracy of our revelations. After some debate, therefore, I called up Sperry, but he flatly refused to go on any further.

"Miss Jeremy has been ill since Monday," he said. "Mrs. Dane's rheumatism is worse, her companion is nervously upset, and your own wife called me up an hour ago and says you are sleeping with a light, and she thinks you ought to go away. The whole club is shot to pieces."

But, although I am a small and not a courageous man, the desire to examine the Wells house clung to me tenaciously. Suppose there were cartridges in his table drawer? Suppose I should find the second bullet hole in the ceiling? I no longer deceived myself by any argument that my interest was purely scientific. There is a point at which curiosity becomes unbearable, when it becomes an obsession, like hunger. I had reached that point.

Nevertheless, I found it hard to plan the necessary deception to my wife. My habits have always been entirely orderly and regular. My wildest dissipation was the Neighborhood Club. I could not recall an evening away from home in years, except on business. Yet now I must have a free evening, possibly an entire night.

In planning for this, I forgot my nervousness for a time. I decided finally to tell my wife that an out-of-town client wished to talk business with me, and that day, at luncheon—I go home to luncheon—I mentioned that such a client was in town.

"It is possible," I said, as easily as I could, "that we may not get through this afternoon. If things should run over into the evening, I'll telephone."

She took it calmly enough, but later on, as I was taking an electric flash from the drawer of the hall table and putting it in my overcoat pocket, she came on me, and I thought she looked surprised.

During the afternoon I was beset with doubts and uneasiness. Suppose she called up my office and found that the client I had named was not in town? It is undoubtedly true that a tangled web we weave when first we practice to deceive, for on my return to the office I was at once quite certain that Mrs. Johnson would telephone and make the inquiry.

After some debate I called my secretary and told her to say, if such a message came in, that Mr. Forbes was in town and that I had an appointment with him. As a matter of fact, no such inquiry came in, but as Miss Joyce, my secretary, knew that Mr. Forbes was in Europe, I was conscious for some months afterward that Miss Joyce's eyes occasionally rested on me in a speculative and suspicious manner.

Other things also increased my uneasiness as the day wore on. There was, for instance, the matter of the back door to the Wells house. Nothing was more unlikely than that the key would still be hanging there. I must, therefore, get a key.

At three o'clock I sent the office-boy out for a backdoor key. He looked so surprised that I explained that we had lost our key, and that I required an assortment of keys of all sizes.

"What sort of key?" he demanded, eyeing me with his feet apart.

"Just an ordinary key," I said. "Not a Yale key. Nothing fancy. Just a plain back-door key." At something after four my wife called up, in great excitement. A boy and a man had been to the house and had fitted an extra key to the back door, which had two excellent ones already. She was quite hysterical and had sent for the police, but the officer had arrived after they had gone.

"They are burglars, of course!" she said. "Burglars often have boys with them, to go through the pantry windows. I'm so nervous I could scream."

I tried to tell her that if the door was unlocked there was no need to use the pantry window, but she rang off quickly and, I thought, coldly. Not, however, before she had said that my plan to spend the evening out was evidently known in the underworld!

By going through my desk I found a number of keys, mostly trunk keys and one the key to a dog collar. But late in the afternoon I visited a client of mine who is in the hardware business, and secured quite a selection. One of them was a skeleton key. He persisted in regarding the matter as a joke, and poked me between the shoulder blades as I went out.

"If you're arrested with all that hardware on you," he said, "you'll be held as a first-class burglar. You are equipped to open anything from a can of tomatoes to the missionary box in church."

But I felt that already, innocent as I was, I was leaving a trail of suspicion behind me: Miss Joyce and the office boy, the dealer and my wife. And I had not started yet.

I dined in a small chop-house where I occasionally lunch, and took a large cup of strong black coffee.

When I went out into the night again I found that a heavy fog had settled down, and I began to feel again something of the strange and disturbing quality of the day which had ended in Arthur Wells's death. Already a potential housebreaker, I avoided policemen, and the very jingling of the keys in my pocket sounded loud and incriminating to my ears.

The Wells house was dark. Even the arc lamp in the street was shrouded in fog. But the darkness, which added to my nervousness, added also to my security.

I turned and felt my way cautiously to the rear of the house. Suddenly I remembered the dog. But of course he was gone. As I cautiously ascended the steps the dead leaves on the vines rattled, as at the light touch of a hand, and I was tempted to turn and run.

I do not like deserted houses. Even in daylight they have a sinister effect on me. They seem, in their empty spaces, to have held and recorded all that has happened in the dusty past. The Wells house that night, looming before me, silent and mysterious, seemed the embodiment of all the deserted houses I had known. Its empty and unshuttered windows were like blind eyes, gazing in, not out.

Nevertheless, now that the time had come, a certain amount of courage came with it. I am not ashamed to confess that a certain part of it came from the anticipation of the Neighborhood Club's plaudits. For Herbert to have made such an investigation, or even Sperry, with his height and his iron muscles, would not have surprised them. But I was aware that while they expected intelligence and even humor, of a sort, from me, they did not anticipate any particular bravery.

The flash was working, but rather feebly. I found the nail where the door-key had formerly hung, but the key, as I had expected, was gone. I was less than five minutes, I fancy, in finding a key from my collection that would fit. The bolt slid back with a click, and the door opened.

It was still early in the evening, eight-thirty or thereabouts. I tried to think of that; to remember that, only a few blocks away, some of my friends were still dining, or making their way into theaters. But the silence of the house came out to meet me on the threshold, and its blackness enveloped me like a wave. It was unfortunate, too, that I remembered just then that it was, or soon would be, the very hour of young Wells's death.

Nevertheless, once inside the house, the door to the outside closed and facing two alternatives, to go on with it or to cut and run, I found a sort of desperate courage, clenched my teeth, and felt for the nearest light switch.

The electric light had been cut off!

I should have expected it, but I had not. I remember standing in the back hall and debating whether to go on or to get out. I was not only in a highly nervous state, but I was also badly handicapped. However, as the moments wore on and I stood there, with the quiet unbroken by no mysterious sounds, I gained a certain confidence. After a short period of readjustment, therefore, I felt my way to the library door, and into the room. Once there, I used the flash to discover that the windows were shuttered, and proceeded to take off my hat and coat, which I placed on a chair near the door. It was at this time that I discovered that the battery of my lamp was very weak, and finding a candle in a tall brass stick on the mantelpiece, I lighted it.

Then I looked about. The house had evidently been hastily closed. Some of the furniture was covered with sheets, while part of it stood unprotected. The rug had been folded into the center of the room and covered with heavy brown papers, and I was extremely startled to hear the papers rustling. A mouse, however, proved to be the source of the sound, and I pulled myself together with a jerk.

It is to be remembered that I had left my hat and overcoat on a chair near the door. There could be no mistake, as the chair was a light one, and the weight of my overcoat threw it back against the wall.

Candle in hand, I stepped out into the hall, and was immediately met by a crash which reverberated through the house. In my alarm my teeth closed on the end of my tongue, with agonizing results, but the sound died away, and I concluded that an upper window had been left open, and that the rising wind had slammed a door. But my morale had been shaken, and I recklessly lighted a second candle and placed it on the table in the hall at the foot of the staircase, to facilitate my exit in case I desired to make a hurried one.

Then I climbed slowly. The fog had apparently made its way into the house, for when, halfway up, I turned and looked down, the candlelight was hardly more than a spark, surrounded by a luminous aura.

I do not know exactly when I began to feel that I

was not alone in the house. It was, I think, when I was on a chair on top of a table in Arthur's room, with my candle upheld to the ceiling. It seemed to me that something was moving stealthily in the room overhead. I stood there, candle upheld, and every faculty I possessed seemed centered in my ears. It was not a footstep. It was a soft and dragging movement. Had I not been near the ceiling I should not have heard it. Indeed, a moment later I was not certain that I *had* heard it.

My chair, on top of the table, was none too securely balanced. I had found what I was looking for, a part of the plaster ornament broken away, and replaced by a whitish substance, not plaster. I got out my penknife and cut away the foreign matter, showing a small hole beneath, a bullet hole if I knew anything about bullet holes.

Then I heard the dragging movement above, and what with alarm and my insecure position, I suddenly overbalanced, chair and all. My head must have struck on the corner of the table, for I was dazed for a few moments. The candle had gone out, of course. I felt for the chair, righted it, and sat down. I was dizzy and I was frightened. I was afraid to move, lest the dragging thing above come down and creep over me in the darkness and smother me.

And sitting there, I remembered the very things I most wished to forget—the black curtain behind Miss Jeremy, the things flung by unseen hands into the room, the way my watch had slid over the table and fallen to the floor.

Since that time I know there is a madness of courage, born of terror. Nothing could be more intolerable than to sit there and wait. It is the same insanity that drove men out of trenches to the charge and almost certain death, rather than to sit and wait for what might come.

In a way, I dare say I charged the upper floor of the house. Recalling the situation from this safe lapse of time, I think that I was in a condition close to frenzy. I know that it did not occur to me to leap down the staircase and escape, and I believe now this was due to a conviction that I was dealing with the supernatural, and that on no account did I dare to turn my back on it. All children and some adults, I am sure, have known this feeling.

Whatever drove me, I know that, candle in hand, and hardly sane, I ran up the staircase, and into the room overhead. It was empty.

As suddenly as my sanity had gone, it returned to me. The sight of two small beds, side by side, a tiny dressing-table, a row of toys on the mantelpiece, was calming. Here was the children's night nursery, a white and placid room which could house nothing hideous.

I was humiliated and ashamed. I, Horace Johnson, a man of dignity and reputation, even in a small way a successful after-dinner speaker, numbering fifty-odd years of logical living to my credit, had been running half-maddened toward a mythical danger from which I had been afraid to run away!

I sat down and mopped my face with my pocket handkerchief.

After a time I got up, and going to a window looked down at the quiet world below. The fog was lifting. Automobiles were making cautious progress along the slippery street. A woman with a basket had stopped under the street light and was rearranging her parcels. The clock of the city hall, visible over the opposite roofs, marked only twenty minutes to nine. It was still early evening—not even midnight, the magic hour of the night.

Somehow that fact reassured me, and I was able to take stock of my surroundings. I realized, for instance, that I stood in the room over Arthur's dressing-room, and that it was into the ceiling under me that the second—or probably the first—bullet had penetrated. I know, as it happens, very little of firearms, but I did realize that a shot from a .45 Colt automatic would have considerable penetrative power. To be exact, that the bullet had probably either lodged itself in a joist, or had penetrated through the flooring and might be somewhere over my head.

But my candle was inadequate for more than the most superficial examination of the ceiling, which presented so far as I could see an unbroken surface. I turned my attention, therefore, to the floor. It was when I was turning the rug back that I recognized the natural and not supernatural origin of the sound which had so startled me. It had been the soft movement of the carpet across the floor boards.

Someone, then, had been there before me—someone who knew what I knew, had reasoned as I reasoned. Someone who, in all probability, still lurked on the upper floor.

Obeying an impulse, I stood erect and called out sharply, "Sperry!" I said. "Sperry!"

There was no answer. I tried again, calling

Herbert. But only my own voice came back to me, and the whistling of the wind through the window I had opened.

My fears, never long in abeyance that night, roused again. I had instantly a conviction that some human figure, sinister and dangerous, was lurking in the shadows of that empty floor, and I remember backing away from the door and standing in the center of the room, prepared for some stealthy, murderous assault. When none came I looked about for a weapon and finally took the only thing in sight, a coal-tongs from the fireplace. Armed with that, I made a cursory round of the near-by rooms but there was no one hiding in them.

I went back to the rug and examined the floor beneath it. I was right. Someone had been there before me. Bits of splintered wood lay about. The second bullet had been fired, had buried itself in the flooring, and had, some five minutes before, been dug out.

Chapter 7

The extraordinary thing about the Arthur Wells story was not his killing. For killing it was. It was the way it was solved.

Here was a young woman, Miss Jeremy, who had not known young Wells, had not known his wife, had, until that first meeting at Mrs. Dane's, never met any member of the Neighborhood Club except Sperry. Yet, but for her, Arthur Wells would have gone to his grave bearing the stigma of moral cowardice, of suicide.

The solution, when it came, was amazing, but remarkably simple. Like most mysteries. I have in my own house, for instance, an example of a great mystery, founded on mere absent-mindedness.

This is what my wife terms the mystery of the fire-tongs.

I had left the Wells house as soon as I had made the discovery in the night nursery. I carried the candle and the fire-tongs downstairs. I was, apparently, calm but watchful. I would have said that I had never been more calm in my life. I knew quite well that I had the fire-tongs in my hand. Just when I ceased to be cognizant of them was probably when, on entering the library, I found that my overcoat had disappeared, and that my stiff hat, badly broken, lay on the floor. However, as I saw, I was still extraordinarily composed. I picked up my hat and moving to the rear door, went out and closed it. When I reached the street, however, I had only gone a few yards when I discovered that I was still carrying the lighted candle, and that a man, passing by, had stopped and was staring after me.

My composure is shown by the fact that I dropped the candle down the next sewer opening, but the fact remains that I carried the fire-tongs home. I do not recall doing so. In fact, I knew nothing of the matter until morning. On the way to my house I was elaborating a story to the effect that my overcoat had been stolen from a restaurant where I and my client had dined. The hat offered more serious difficulties. I fancied that, by kissing my wife good-by at the breakfast table, I might be able to get out without her following me to the front door, which is her custom.

But, as a matter of fact, I need not have concerned myself about the hat. When I descended to breakfast the next morning I found her surveying the umbrella stand in the hall. The fire-tongs were standing there, gleaming, among my sticks and umbrellas.

I lied. I lied shamelessly. She is a nervous woman, and, as we have no children, her attitude toward me is one of watchful waiting. Through long years she has expected me to commit some indiscretion—innocent, of course, such as going out without my overcoat on a cool day—and she intends to be on hand for every emergency. I dared not confess, therefore, that on the previous evening I had burglariously entered a closed house, had there surprised another intruder at work, had fallen and bumped my head severely, and had, finally, had my overcoat taken.

"Horace," she said coldly, "where did you get those fire-tongs?"

"Fire-tongs?" I repeated. "Why, that's so. They *are* fire-tongs."

"Where did you get them?"

"My dear," I expostulated, "*I* get them?"

"What I would like to ask," she said, with an icy calmness that I have learned to dread, "is whether you carried them home over your head, under the impression that you had your umbrella."

"Certainly not," I said with dignity. "I assure you, my dear—"

"I am not a curious woman," she put in incisively, "but when my husband spends an evening out, and returns minus his overcoat, with his hat mashed, a lump the size of an egg over his ear, and puts a pair of fire-tongs in the umbrella stand under the impression that it is an umbrella, I have a right to ask at least if he intends to continue his life of debauchery."

I made a mistake then, I should have told her. Instead, I took my broken hat and jammed it on my head with a force that made the lump she had noticed jump like a toothache, and went out.

When, at noon and luncheon, I tried to tell her the truth, she listened to the end. Then: "I should think you could have done better than that," she said. "You have had all morning to think it out."

However, if things were in a state of armed neutrality at home, I had a certain compensation for them when I told my story to Sperry that afternoon.

"You see how it is," I finished. "You can stay out of this, or come in, Sperry, but I cannot stop now. He was murdered beyond a doubt, and there is an intelligent effort being made to eliminate every particle of evidence."

He nodded. "It looks like it. And this man who was there last night—"

"Why a man?"

"He took your overcoat, instead of his own, didn't he? It may have been—it's curious, isn't it, that we've had no suggestion of Ellingham in all the rest of the material."

Like the other members of the Neighborhood Club, he had a copy of the proceedings at the two seances, and now he brought them out and fell to studying them.

"She was right about the bullet in the ceiling," he reflected. "I suppose you didn't look for the box of shells for the revolver?"

"I meant to, but it slipped my mind."

He shuffled the loose pages of the record. "Cane—washed away by the water—a knee that is hurt—the curtain would have been safer—Hawkins—the drawing-room furniture is all over the house. That last, Horace, isn't pertinent. It refers clearly to the room we were in. Of course, the point is, how much of the rest is also extraneous matter?" He re-read one of the sheets. "Of course that belongs, about Hawkins. And probably this: 'It will be terrible if the letters are

187

found.' They were in the pocketbook, presumably."

He folded up the papers and replaced them in a drawer.

"We'd better go back to the house," he said. "Whoever took your overcoat by mistake probably left one. The difficulty is, of course, that he probably discovered his error and went back again last night. Confound it, man, if you had thought of that at the time, we would have something to go on today."

"If I had thought of a number of things I'd have stayed out of the place altogether," I retorted tartly. "I wish you could help me about the fire-tongs, Sperry. I don't seem able to think of any explanation that Mrs. Johnson would be willing to accept."

"Tell her the truth."

"I don't think you understand," I explained. "She simply wouldn't believe it. And if she did I should have to agree to drop the investigation. As a matter of fact, Sperry, I resorted to subterfuge in order to remain out last evening, and I am bitterly regretting my mendacity."

But Sperry has, I am afraid, rather loose ideas.

"Every man," he said, "would rather tell the truth, but every woman makes it necessary to lie to her. Forget the fire-tongs, Horace, and forget Mrs. Johnson tonight. He may not have dared to go back in daylight for his overcoat."

"Very well," I agreed.

But it was not very well, and I knew it. I felt that, in a way, my whole domestic happiness was at stake. My wife is a difficult person to argue with, and as tenacious of an opinion once formed as are all very amiable people. However, unfortunately for our investigation, but luckily for me under the circumstances, Sperry was called to another city that afternoon and did not return for two days.

It was, it will be recalled, on the Thursday night following the second sitting that I had gone alone to the Wells house, and my interview with Sperry was on Friday. It was on Friday afternoon that I received a telephone message from Mrs. Dane.

It was actually from her secretary, the Clara who had recorded the seances. It was Mrs. Dane's misfortune to be almost entirely dependent on the various young women who, one after the other, were employed to look after her. I say "one after the other" advisedly. It had long been a matter of good-natured jesting in the Neighborhood Club that Mrs. Dane conducted a matrimonial bureau, as one young woman after another was married from her house. It was her kindly habit, on such occasions, to give the bride a wedding, and only a month before it had been my privilege to give away in holy wedlock Miss Clara's predecessor.

"Mrs. Dane would like you to stop in and have a cup of tea with her this afternoon, Mr. Johnson," said the secretary.

"At what time?"

"At four o'clock."

I hesitated. I felt that my wife was waiting at home for further explanation of the coal-tongs, and that the sooner we had it out the better. But, on the other hand, Mrs. Dane's invitations, by reason of her infirmity, took on something of the nature of commands.

"Please say that I will be there at four," I replied.

I bought a new hat that afternoon, and told the clerk to destroy the old one. Then I went to Mrs. Dane's.

She was in the drawing-room, now restored to its usual clutter of furniture and ornaments. I made my way around two tables, stepped over a hassock and under the leaves of an artificial palm, and shook her hand.

She was plainly excited. Never have I known a woman who, confined to a wheel-chair, lived so hard. She did not allow life to pass her windows, if I may put it that way. She called it in, and set it moving about her chair, herself the nucleus around which were enacted all sorts of small neighborhood dramas and romances. Her secretaries did not marry. She married them.

It is curious to look back and remember how Herbert and Sperry and myself had ignored this quality in her, in the Wells case. She was not to be ignored, as I discovered that afternoon.

"Sit down," she said. "You look half sick, Horace."

Nothing escapes her eyes, so I was careful to place myself with the lump on my head turned away from her. But I fancy she saw it, for her eyes twinkled.

"Horace! Horace!" she said. "How I have detested you all week!"

"I? You detested me?"

"Loathed you," she said with unction. "You are cruel and ungrateful. Herbert has influenza, and does not count. And Sperry is in love—oh yes, I know it. I know a great many things. But you!"

I could only stare at her.

"The strange thing is," she went on, "that I have known you for years, and never suspected your sense of humor. You'll forgive me, I know, if I tell you that your lack of humor was to my mind the only flaw in an otherwise perfect character."

"I am not aware—" I began stiffly. "I have always believed that I furnished to the Neighborhood Club its only leaven of humor."

"Don't spoil it," she begged. "Don't. If you could know how I have enjoyed it. All afternoon I have been chuckling. The fire-tongs, Horace. The fire-tongs!"

Then I knew that my wife had been to Mrs. Dane and I drew a long breath. "I assure you," I said gravely, "that while doubtless I carried the wretched things home and—er—placed them where they were found, I have not the slightest recollection of it. And it is hardly amusing, is it?"

"Amusing!" she cried. "It's delicious. It has made me a young woman again. Horace, if I could have seen your wife's face when she found them, I would give cheerfully almost anything I possess."

But underneath her mirth I knew there was something else. And, after all, she could convince my wife if she were convinced herself. I told the whole story—of the visit Sperry and I had made the night Arthur Wells was shot, and of what we discovered; of the clerk at the pharmacy and his statement, and even of the whisky and its unfortunate effect—at which, I regret to say, she was vastly amused; and, last of all, of my experience the previous night in the deserted house.

She was very serious when I finished. Tea came,

191

but we forgot to drink it. Her eyes flashed with excitement, her faded face flushed. And, with it all, as I look back, there was an air of suppressed excitement that seemed to have nothing to do with my narrative. I remembered it, however, when the dénouement came the following week.

She was a remarkable woman. Even then she knew, or strongly suspected, the thing that the rest of us had missed, the x of the equation. But I think it only fair to record that she was in possession of facts which we did not have, and which she did not divulge until the end.

"You have been so ungenerous with me," she said finally, "that I am tempted not to tell you why I sent for you. Of course, I know I am only a helpless old woman, and you men are people of affairs. But now and then I have a flash of intelligence. I'm going to tell you, but you don't deserve it."

She went down into the black silk bag at her side which was as much a part of her attire as the false front she wore with such careless abandon, and which, brown in color and indifferently waved, was invariably parting from its mooring. She drew out a newspaper clipping.

"On going over Clara's notes," she said, "I came to the conclusion, last Tuesday, that the matter of the missing handbag and the letters was important. More important, probably, then the mere record shows. Do you recall the note of distress in Miss Jeremy's voice? It was almost a wail."

I had noticed it.

"I have plenty of time to think," she added, not without pathos. "There is only one Monday night in

192

the week, and—the days are long. It occurred to me to try to trace that bag."

"In what way?"

"How does anyone trace lost articles?" she demanded. "By advertising, of course. Last Wednesday I advertised for the bag."

I was too astonished to speak.

"I reasoned like this: If there was no such bag, there was no harm done. As a matter of fact, if there was no such bag, the chances were that we were all wrong, anyhow. If there was such a bag, I wanted it. Here is the advertisement as I inserted it."

She gave me a small newspaper cutting:

Lost, a handbag containing private letters, car-tickets, etc. Liberal reward paid for its return. Please write to A 31, the Daily News.

I sat with it on my palm. It was so simple, so direct. And I, a lawyer, and presumably reasonably acute, had not thought of it!

"You are wasted on us, Mrs. Dane," I acknowledged. "Well? I see something has come of it."

"Yes, but I'm not ready for it."

She dived again into the bag, and brought up another clipping.

"On the day that I had that inserted," she said impressively, "this also appeared. They were in the same column." She read the second clipping aloud, slowly, that I might gain all its significance:

Lost on the night of Monday, November the second, between State Avenue and Park Avenue, a black handbag containing keys, car-tickets, private letters, and a small sum of money. Reward and no questions asked if returned to Daily News office.

She passed the clipping to me and I compared the two. It looked strange, and I confess to a tingling feeling that coincidence, that element so much to be feared in any investigation, was not the solution here. But there was such a chance, and I spoke of it.

"Coincidence rubbish!" she retorted. "I am not through, my friend."

She went down into the bag again, and I expected nothing less than the pocketbook, letters and all, to appear. But she dragged up, among a miscellany of handkerchiefs, a bottle of smelling-salts, and a few almonds, of which she was inordinately fond, an envelope.

"Yesterday," she said, "I took a taxicab ride. You know my chair gets tiresome occasionally. I stopped at the newspaper office, and found the bag had not been turned in, but that there was a letter for A 31." She held out the envelope to me.

"Read it," she observed. "It is a curious human document. You'll probably be no wiser for reading it, but it shows one thing: We are on the track of something."

I have the letter before me now. It is written on glazed paper, ruled with blue lines. The writing is of the flowing style we used to call Spencerian, and if it lacks character I am inclined to believe that its weakness is merely the result of infrequent use of a pen:

You know who this is from. I have the bag and the letters. In a safe place. If you would treat me like a human being, you could have them. I know where the walking-stick is, also. I will tell you this. I have no wish to do her any harm. She will have to pay up in the next world, even if she gets off in this. The way I reason is this: As long as I have the things, I've got the whip-hand. I've got you, too, although you may think I haven't.

About the other matter, I was innocent. I swear it again. I never did it. You are the only one in all the world. I would rather be dead than go on like this.

It is unsigned.

I stared from the letter to Mrs. Dane. She was watching me, her face grave and rather sad.

"You and I, Horace," she said, "live our orderly lives. We eat, and sleep, and talk, and even labor. We think we are living. But for the last day or two I have been seeing visions—you and I and the rest of us, living on the surface, and underneath, carefully kept down so it will not make us uncomfortable, a world of passion and crime and violence and suffering. That letter is a tragedy."

But if she had any suspicion then as to the writer, and I think she had not, she said nothing, and soon after I started for home. I knew that one of two things would have happened there: either my wife would have put away the fire-tongs, which would indicate a truce, or they would remain as they had been, which would indicate that she still waited for the explanation I could not give. It was with a certain tension, therefore, that I opened my front door.

The fire-tongs still stood in the stand.

In one way, however, Mrs. Johnson's refusal to speak to me that evening had a certain value, for it enabled me to leave the house without explanation, and thus to discover that, if an overcoat had been left in place of my own, it had been taken away. It also gave me an opportunity to return the fire-tongs, a proceeding which I had considered would assist in a return of the *entente cordiale* at home, but which most unjustly appeared to have exactly the opposite effect.

It has been my experience that the most innocent action may, under certain circumstances, assume an appearance of extreme guilt. . . .

By Saturday the condition of affairs between my wife and myself remained *in statu quo*, and I had decided on a bold step. This was to call a special meeting of the Neighborhood Club, without Miss Jeremy, and put before them the situation as it stood at that time, with a view to formulating a future course of action, and also of publicly vindicating myself before my wife.

In deference to Herbert Robinson's recent attack of influenza, we met at the Robinson house. Sperry himself wheeled Mrs. Dane over, and made a speech.

"We have called this meeting," he said, "because a rather singular situation has developed. What was commenced purely as an interesting experiment has gone beyond that stage. We find ourselves in the curious position of taking what comes very close to being a part in a domestic tragedy. The affair is made more delicate by the fact that this tragedy involved people who, if not our friends, as least are very well known to us. The purpose of this meeting, to be brief, is to determine whether the Neighborhood Club, as a body, wishes to go on with the investigation, or to stop where we are."

He paused, but, as no one spoke, he went on again. "It is really not as simple as that," he said. "To stop now, in view of the evidence we intend to place before the Club, is to leave in all our minds certain suspicions that may be entirely unjust. On the other hand, to go on is very possibly to place us all in a position where to keep silent is to be an accessory after a crime."

He then proceeded, in orderly fashion, to review the first sitting and its results. He read from notes, elaborating them as he went along, for the benefit of the women, who had not been fully informed. As all the data of the Club is now in my possession, I copy these notes.

"I shall review briefly the first sitting, and what followed it." He read the notes of the sitting first. "You will notice that I have made no comment on the physical phenomena which occurred early in the seance. This is for two reasons: first, it has no bearing on the question at issue. Second, it has no quality of novelty. Certain people, under certain conditions, are able to exert powers that we can not explain. I have no belief whatever in their spiritistic quality. They are purely physical, the exercise of powers we have either not yet risen high enough in our scale of development to recognize generally, or which have survived from some early period when our natural gifts had not been smothered by civilization."

197

And, to make our position clear, that is today the attitude of the Neighborhood Club. The supernormal, as I said at the beginning, not the supernatural, is our explanation.

Sperry's notes were alphabetical.

(a) At 9:15, or somewhat earlier, on Monday night a week ago Arthur Wells killed himself, or was killed. At 9:30 on that same evening by Mr. Johnson's watch, consulted at the time, Miss Jeremy had described such a crime. (Here he elaborated, repeating the medium's account.)

(b) At midnight, Sperry, reaching home, had found a message summoning him to the Wells house. The message had been left at 9:35. He had telephoned me, and we had gone together, arriving at approximately 12:30.

(c) We had been unable to enter, and, recalling the medium's description of a key on a nail among the vines, had searched for and found such a key, and had admitted ourselves. Mrs. Wells, a governess, a doctor, and two policemen were in the house. The dead man lay in the room in which he had died. (Here he went at length into the condition of the room, the revolver with one chamber empty, and the blood-stained sponge and razorstrop behind the bathtub. We had made a hasty examination of the ceiling, but had found no trace of a second shot.

(d) The governess had come in at 9:15, just after the death. Mr. Horace Johnson had had a talk with her. She had left the front door unfastened when she went out at eight o'clock. She said she had gone out to telephone about another position, as she was dissatisfied. She had phoned from Elliott's pharmacy on State Avenue. Later that night Mr. Johnson had gone to Elliott's. She had lied about the message. She had really telephoned to a number which the pharmacy clerk had already discovered was that of the Ellingham house. The message was that Mr. Ellingham was not to come, as Mr. and Mrs. Wells were going out. It was not the first time she had telephoned to that number.

There was a stir in the room. Something which we had tacitly avoided had come suddenly into the open. Sperry raised his hand.

"It is necessary to be explicit," he said, "that the Club may see where it stands. It is, of course, not necessary to remind ourselves that this evening's disclosures are of the most secret nature. I urge that the Club jump to no hasty conclusions, and that there shall be no interruptions until we have finished with our records."

(e) At a private seance, which Mr. Johnson and I decided was excusable under the circumstances, the medium was unable to give us anything. This in spite of the fact that we had taken with us a walking-stick belonging to the dead man.

(f) The second sitting of the Club. I need only refresh your minds as to one or two things; the medium spoke of a lost pocketbook, and of letters. While the point is at least capable of doubt, apparently the letters were in the pocketbook. Also, she said that a *curtain* would have been better, that Hawkins was a nuisance, and that everything was all right unless the bullet had made a hole in the floor above. You will also recall the mention of a box of cartridges in a table drawer in Arthur Wells's room.

"I will now ask Mr. Horace Johnson to tell what occurred on the night before last, Thursday evening."

"I do not think Horace has a very clear recollection of last Thursday night," my wife said, coldly. "And I wish to go on record at once that if he claims that spirits broke his hat, stole his overcoat, bumped his head and sent him home with a pair of fire-tongs for a walking-stick, I don't believe him."

Which attitude Herbert, I regret to say, did not help when he said:

"Don't worry, Horace will soon be too old for the gay life. Remember your arteries, Horace."

I have quoted this interruption to show how little, outside of Sperry, Mrs. Dane and myself, the Neighborhood Club appreciated the seriousness of the situation. Herbert, for instance, had been greatly amused when Sperry spoke of my finding the razorstrop and had almost chuckled over our investigation of the ceiling.

But they were very serious when I had finished my statement.

"Great Scott!" Herbert said. "Then she was right,

after all! I say, I guess I've been no end of an ass."

I was inclined to agree with him. But the real effect of my brief speech was on my wife.

It was a real compensation for that night of terror and for the uncomfortable time since to find her gaze no longer cold, but sympathetic, and—if I may be allowed to say so—admiring. When at last I sat down beside her, she put her hand on my arm in a way that I had missed since the unfortunate affair of the pharmacy whisky.

Mrs. Dane then read and explained the two clippings and the letter, and the situation, so far as it had developed, was before the Club.

Were we to go on, or to stop?

Put to a vote, the women were for going on. The men were more doubtful, and Herbert voiced what I think we all felt.

"We're getting in pretty deep," he said, "We have no right to step in where the law has stepped out—no legal right, that is. As to moral right, it depends on what we are holding these sittings for. If we are making what we started out to make, an investigation into psychic matters, then we can go on. But with this proviso, I think: Whatever may come of it, the result is of psychic interest only. We are not trailing a criminal."

"Crime is the affair of every decent-minded citizen," his sister put in concisely.

But the general view was that Herbert was right. I am not defending our course. I am recording it. It is, I admit, open to argument.

Having decided on what to do or not to do, we broke into animated discussion. The letter to A 31 was the rock on which all our theories foundered, that and the message the governess had sent to Charlie Ellingham not to come to the Wells house that night. By no stretch of rather excited imaginations could we imagine Ellingham writing such a letter. Who had written the letter, then, and for whom was it meant?

As to the telephone message, it seemed to preclude the possibility of Ellingham's having gone to the house that night. But the fact remained that a man, as yet unidentified, was undoubtedly concerned in the case, had written the letter, and had probably been in the Wells house the night I went there alone.

In the end, we decided to hold one more seance, and then, unless the further developments were such that we must go on, to let the affair drop.

It is typical of the strained nervous tension which had developed in all of us during the past twelve days, that that night when, having forgotten to let the dog in, my wife and I were roused from a sound sleep by his howling, she would not allow me to go down and admit him.

Chapter 8

On Sunday I went to church. I felt, after the strange phenomena in Mrs. Dane's drawing-room, and after the contact with tragedy to which they had led, that I must hold with a sort of desperation to the traditions and beliefs by which I had hitherto regulated my conduct. And the church did me good. Between the immortality it taught and the theory of spiritualism as we had seen it in action there was a great gulf, and I concluded that this gulf was the soul. The conclusion that mind and certain properties of mind survived was not enough. The thought of a disembodied intelligence was pathetic, depressing. But the thought of a glorified soul was the hope of the world. . . .

My wife, too, was in a penitent and rather exalted mood. During the sermon she sat with her hand in mine, and I was conscious of peace and a deep thankfulness. We had been married for many years, and we had grown very close. Of what importance was the Wells case, or what mattered is that there were strange new-old laws in the universe, so long as we kept together?

That my wife had felt a certain bitterness toward Miss Jeremy, a jealousy of her powers, even of her youth, had not dawned on me. But when, in her new humility, she suggested that we call on the medium that afternoon, I realized that, in her own way, she was making a sort of atonement.

Miss Jeremy lived with an elderly spinster cousin, a short distance out of town. It was a grim house, coldly and rigidly Calvinistic. It gave an unpleasant impression at the start, and our comfort was not increased by the discovery, made early in the call, that the cousin regarded the Neighborhood Club and its members with suspicion.

The cousin—her name was Connell—was small and sharp, and she entered the room followed by a train of cats. All the time she was frigidly greeting us, cats were coming in at the door, one after the other. It fascinated me. I do not like cats. I am, as a matter of confession, afraid of cats. They affect me as do snakes. They trailed in in a seemingly endless procession, and one of them took a fancy to me, and leaped from behind onto my shoulder. The shock set me stammering.

"My cousin is out," said Miss Connell. "Doctor Sperry has taken her for a ride. She will be back very soon."

I shook a cat from my trouser leg, and my wife made an unimportant remark.

"I may as well tell you, I disapprove of what Alice is doing," said Miss Connell. "She doesn't have to. I've offered her a good home. She was brought up a

Presbyterian. I call this sort of thing playing with the powers of darkness. Only the eternally damned are doomed to walk the earth. The blessed are at rest."

"But you believe in her powers, don't you?" my wife asked.

"I believe she can do extraordinary things. She saw my father's spirit in this very room last night, and described him, although she had never seen him."

As she had said that only the eternally damned were doomed to walk the earth, I was tempted to comment on this stricture on her departed parent, but a large cat, much scarred with fighting and named Violet, insisted at that moment on crawling into my lap, and my attention was distracted.

"But the whole thing is un-Christian and undignified," Miss Connell proceeded, in her cold voice. "Come, Violet, don't annoy the gentleman. I have other visions of the next life than of rapping on tables and chairs, and throwing small articles about."

It was an extraordinary visit. Even the arrival of Miss Jeremy herself, flushed with the air and looking singularly normal, was hardly a relief. Sperry, who followed, was clearly pleased to see us, however.

It was not hard to see how things were with him. He helped the girl out of her wraps with a manner that was almost proprietary, and drew a chair for her close to the small fire which hardly affected the chill of the room.

With their entrance a spark of hospitality seemed to kindle in the cat lady's breast. It was evident that she liked Sperry. Perhaps she saw in him a method of weaning her cousin from traffic with the powers of darkness. She said something about tea, and went out.

Sperry looked across at the girl and smiled.

"Shall I tell them?" he said.

"I want very much to have them know."

He stood up, and with that unconscious drama which actuates a man at a crisis in his affairs, he put a hand on her shoulder. "This young lady is going to marry me," he said. "We are very happy today."

But I thought he eyed us anxiously. We were very close friends, and he wanted our approval. I am not sure if we were wise. I do not yet know. But something of the new understanding between my wife and myself must have found its way to our voices, for he was evidently satisfied.

"Then *that's* all right," he said heartily. And my wife, to my surprise, kissed the girl.

Except for the cats, sitting around, the whole thing was strangely normal. And yet, even there, something happened that set me to thinking afterward. Not that it was strange in itself, but that it seemed never possible to get very far away from the Wells mystery.

Tea was brought in by Hawkins!

I knew him immediately, but he did not at once see me. He was evidently accustomed to seeing Sperry there, and he did not recognize my wife. But when he had put down the tray and turned to pick up Sperry's overcoat to carry it into the hall, he saw me. The man actually started. I cannot say that he changed color. He was always a pale, anemic-looking individual. But it was a perceptible instant before he stopped and gathered up the coat.

Sperry turned to me when he had gone out. "That

was Hawkins, Horace," he said. "You remember, don't you? The Wellses' butler."

"I knew him at once."

"He wrote to me asking for a position, and I got him this. Looks sick, poor devil. I intend to have a go at his chest."

"How long has he been here?"

"More than a week, I think."

As I drank my tea, I pondered. After all, the Neighborhood Club must guard against the possibility of fraud, and I felt that Sperry had been indiscreet, to say the least. From the time of Hawkins's service in Miss Jeremy's home there would always be the suspicion of collusion between them. I did not believe it was so, but Herbert, for instance, would be inclined to suspect her. Suppose that Hawkins knew about the crime? Or knew something and surmised the rest?

When we rose to go Sperry drew me aside.

"You think I've made a mistake?"

"I do."

He flung away with an impatient gesture, then came back to me.

"Now look here," he said, "I know what you mean, and the whole idea is absurd. Of course I never thought about it, but even allowing for connivance—which I don't for a moment—the fellow was not in the house at the time of the murder."

"I know he *says* he was not."

"Even then," he said, "how about the first sitting? I'll swear she had never even heard of him then."

"The fact remains that his presence here makes us all absurd."

"Do you want me to throw him out?"

"I don't see what possible good that will do now."

I was uneasy, all the way home. The element of doubt, always so imminent in our dealings with psychic phenomena, had me by the throat. How much did Hawkins know? Was there any way, without going to the police, to find if he had really been out of the Wells house that night, now almost two weeks ago, when Arthur Wells had been killed?

That evening I went to Sperry's house, after telephoning that I was coming. On the way I stopped in at Mrs. Dane's and secured something from her. She was wildly curious, and made me promise to go in on my way back, and explain. I made a compromise.

"I will come in if I have anything to tell you," I said.

But I knew, by her grim smile, that she would station herself by her window, and that I would stop, unless I made a detour of three blocks to avoid her. She is a very determined woman.

Sperry was waiting for me in his library, a pleasant room which I have often envied him. Even the most happily married man wishes, now and then, for some quiet, dull room which is essentially his own. My own library is really the family sitting-room, and a Christmas or so ago my wife presented me with a very handsome phonograph instrument. My reading, therefore, is done to music, and the necessity for putting my book down to change the record at times interferes somewhat with my train of thought.

So I entered Sperry's library with appreciation. He

was standing by the fire, with the grave face and slightly bent head of his professional manner. We say, in the neighborhood, that Sperry uses his professional manner as armor, so I was rather prepared to do battle; but he forestalled me.

"Horce," he said, "I have been a fool, a driveling idiot. We were getting something at those sittings. Something real. She's wonderful. She's going to give it up, but the fact remains that she has some power we haven't, and now I've discredited her! I see it plainly enough." He was rather bitter about it, but not hostile. His fury was at himself. "Of course," he went on, "I am sure that she got nothing from Hawkins. But the fact remains—" He was hurt in his pride of her.

"I wonder," I said, "if you kept the letter Hawkins wrote you when he asked for a position."

He was not sure. He went into his consulting room and was gone for some time. I took the opportunity to glance over his books and over the room.

Arthur Wells's stick was standing in a corner, and I took it up and examined it. It was an English malacca, light and strong, and had seen service. It was long, too long for me; it occurred to me that Wells had been about my height, and that it was odd that he should have carried so long a stick. There was no ease in swinging it.

From that to the memory of Hawkins's face when Sperry took it, the night of the murder, in the hall of the Wells house, was only a step. I seemed that day to be thinking considerably about Hawkins.

When Sperry returned I laid the stick on the table.

There can be no doubt that I did so, for I had to move a book-rack to place it. One end, the handle, was near the ink-well, and the ferrule lay on a copy of Gibson's *Life Beyond the Grave*, which Sperry had evidently been reading.

Sperry had found the letter. As I glanced at it I recognized the writing at once, thin and rather sexless, Spencerian:

> *Dear Sir: Since Mr. Wells's death I am out of employment. Before I took the position of butler with Mr. Wells I was valet to Mr. Ellingham, and before that, in England, to Lord Condray. I have a very good letter of recommendation from Lord Condray. If you need a servant at this time I would do my best to give satisfaction.*
>
> (Signed) ARTHUR HAWKINS.

I put down the application, and took the anonymous letter about the bag from my pocketbook. "Read this, Sperry," I said. "You know the letter. Mrs. Dane read it to us Saturday night. But compare the writing."

He compared the two, with a slight lifting of his eyebrows. Then he put them down. "Hawkins!" he said. "Hawkins has the letters! And the bag!"

"Exactly," I commented dryly. "In other words, Hawkins was in Miss Jeremy's house when, at the second sitting, she told of the letters."

I felt rather sorry for Sperry. He paced the room wretchedly, the two letters in his hand.

"But why should he tell her, if he did?" he demanded. "The writer of that anonymous letter was writing for only one person. Every effort is made to conceal his identity."

I felt that he was right. The point was well taken.

"The question now is, to whom was it written?"

We pondered that, to no effect. That Hawkins had certain letters which touched on the Wells affair, that they were probably in his possession in the Connell house, was clear enough. But we had no possible authority for trying to get the letters, although Sperry was anxious to make the attempt.

"Although I feel," he said, "that it is too late to help her very much. She is innocent; I know that. I think you know that, too, deep in that legal mind of yours. It is wrong to discredit her because I did a foolish thing." He warmed to his argument. "Why, think, man," he said. "The whole first sitting was practically coincident with the crime itself."

It was true enough. Whatever suspicion might be cast on the second seance, the first at least remained inexplicable, by any laws we recognized. In a way, I felt sorry for Sperry. Here he was, on the first day of his engagement, protesting her honesty, her complete ignorance of the revelations she had made and his intention to keep her in ignorance, and yet betraying his own anxiety and possible doubt in the same breath.

"She did not even know there was a family named Wells. When I said that Hawkins had been employed by the Wells, it meant nothing to her. I was watching."

211

So even Sperry was watching. He was in love with her, but his scientific mind, like my legal one, was slow to accept what during the past two weeks it had been asked to accept.

I left him at ten o'clock. Mrs. Dane was still at her window, and her far-sighted old eyes caught me as I tried to steal past. She rapped on the window, and I was obliged to go in. Obliged, too, to tell her of the discovery and, at last, of Hawkins being in the Connell house.

"I want those letters, Horace," she said at last.

"So do I. I'm not going to steal them."

"The question is, where has he got them?"

"The question is, dear lady, that they are not ours to take."

"They are not his, either."

Well, that was true enough. But I had done all the private investigating I cared to. And I told her so. She only smiled cryptically. . . .

So far as I know, Mrs. Dane was the only one among us who had entirely escaped certain strange phenomena during that period, and as I have only so far recorded my own experiences, I shall here place in order the various manifestations made to the other members of the Neighborhood Club during that trying period and in their own words. As none of them have suffered since, a certain allowance must be made for our nervous strain. As before, I shall offer no explanation.

Alice Robinson: On night following second seance saw a light in room, not referable to any outside influence. Was an amorphous body which glowed

212

pallidly and moved about wall over fireplace, gradually coming to stop in a corner, where it faded and disappeared.

Clara——, Mrs. Dane's secretary: Had not slept much since first seance. Was frequently conscious that she was not alone in room, but on turning on light room was always empty. Wakened twice with sense of extreme cold. (I have recorded my own similar experience.)

Sperry has consistently maintained that he had no experiences whatever during that period, but admits that he heard various knockings in his bedroom at night, which he attributed to the lighting of his furnace, and the resulting expansion of the furniture due to heat.

Herbert Robinson: Herbert was the most difficult member of the Club from whom to secure data, but he has recently confessed that he was wakened one night by the light falling on to his bed from a picture which hung on the wall over his mantelpiece, and which stood behind a clock, two glass vases and a pair of candlesticks. The door of his room was locked at the time.

Mrs. Johnson: Had a great many minor disturbances, so that on rousing one night to find me closing a window against a storm she thought I was a specter, and to this day insists that I only entered her room when I heard her scream. For this reason I have made no record of her various experiences, as I felt that her nervous condition precluded accurate observation.

As in all records of psychic phenomena, the

human element must be considered, and I do not attempt either to analyze these various phenomena or to explain them. Herbert, for instance, has been known to walk in his sleep. But I respectfully offer, as opposed to this, that my watch has never been known to walk at all, and that Mrs. Johnson's bracelet could hardly be accused of an attack of nerves.

Chapter 9

The following day was Monday. When I came downstairs I found a neat bundle lying in the hall, and addressed to me. My wife had followed me down, and we surveyed it together.

I had a curious feeling about the parcel, and was for cutting the cord with my knife. But my wife is careful about string. She has always fancied that the time would come when we would need some badly, and it would not be around. I have an entire drawer of my chiffonier, which I really need for other uses, filled with bundles of twine, pink, white and brown. I recall, on one occasion, packing a suitcase in the dusk, in great haste, and emptying the drawer containing my undergarments into it, to discover, when I opened it on the train for my pajamas, nothing but rolls of cord and several packages of Christmas ribbons. So I was obliged to wait until she had untied the knots by means of a hairpin.

It was my overcoat! My overcoat, apparently uninjured, but with the collection of keys I had made missing.

The address was printed, not written, in a large, strong hand, with a stub pen. I did not, at the time, notice the loss of certain papers which had been in the breast pocket. I am rather absent-minded, and it was not until the night after the third sitting that they were recalled to my mind.

At something after eleven Herbert Robinson called me up at my office. He was at Sperry's house, Sperry having been his physician during his recent illness.

"I say, Horace, this is Herbert."

"Yes. How are you?"

"Doing well, Sperry says. I'm at his place now. I'm speaking for him. He's got a patient."

"Yes."

"You were here last night, he says." Herbert has a circumlocutory manner over the phone which irritates me. He begins slowly and does not know how to stop. Talk with him drags on endlessly.

"Well, I admit it," I snapped. "It's not a secret."

He lowered his voice. "Do you happen to have noticed a walking-stick in the library when you were here?"

"Which walking-stick?"

"You know. The one we—"

"Yes. I saw it."

"You didn't, by any chance, take it home with you?"

"No."

"Are you sure?"

"Certainly I'm sure."

"You are an absent-minded beggar, you know," he explained. "You remember about the fire-tongs. And a stick is like an umbrella. One is likely to pick it up and—"

"One is not likely to do anything of the sort. At least, I didn't."

"Oh, all right. Everyone well?"

"Very well, thanks."

"Suppose we'll see you tonight?"

"Not unless you ring off and let me do some work," I said irritably.

He rang off. I was ruffled, I admit; but I was uneasy, also. To tell the truth, the affair of the fire-tongs had cost me my self-confidence. I called up my wife, and she said Herbert was a fool and Sperry also. But she made an exhaustive search of the premises, without result. Whoever had taken the stick, I was cleared. Cleared, at least, for a time. There were strange developments coming that threatened my peace of mind.

It was that day that I discovered that I was being watched. Shadowed, I believe is the technical word. I dare say I had been followed from my house, but I had not noticed. When I went out to lunch a youngish man in a dark overcoat was waiting for the elevator, and I saw him again when I came out of my house. We went downtown again on the same car.

Perhaps I would have thought nothing of it, had I not been summoned to the suburbs on a piece of business concerning a mortgage. He was at the far end of the platform as I took the train to return to the city, with his back to me. I lost him in the crowd at the downtown station, but he evidently had not lost me, for, stopping to buy a newspaper, I turned, and, as my pause had evidently been unexpected, he almost ran into me.

With that tendency of any man who finds himself under suspicion to search his past for some dereliction, possibly forgotten, I puzzled over the situation for some time that afternoon. I did not connect it with the Wells case, for in that matter I was indisputably the hunter, not the hunted.

Although I found no explanation for the matter, I did not tell my wife that evening. Women are strange and she would, I feared, immediately jump to the conclusion that there was something in my private life that I was keeping from her.

Almost all women, I have found, although not overconscious themselves of the charm and attraction of their husbands, are of the conviction that these husbands exert a dangerous fascination over other women, and that this charm, which does not reveal itself in the home circle, is used abroad with occasionally disastrous effect.

My preoccupation, however, did not escape my wife, and she commented on it at dinner.

"You are generally dull, Horace," she said, "but tonight you are deadly."

After dinner I went into our reception room, which is not lighted unless we are expecting guests, and peered out of the window. The detective, or whoever he might be, was walking negligently up the street.

As that was the night of the third seance, I find that my record covers the fact that Mrs. Dane was housecleaning, for which reason we had not been asked to dinner, that my wife and I dined early, at six-thirty, and that it was seven o'clock when Sperry called me by telephone.

"Can you come to my office at once?" he asked. "I dare say Mrs. Johnson won't mind going to the Dane house alone."

"Is there anything new?"

"No. But I want to get into the Wells house again. Bring the keys."

"They were in the overcoat. It came back today, but the keys are missing."

"Did you lock the back door?"

"I don't remember. No, of course not. I didn't have the keys."

"Then there's a chance," he observed, after a moment's pause. "Anyhow, it's worth trying. Herbert told you about the stick?"

"Yes. I never had it, Sperry."

Fortunately, during this conversation my wife was upstairs dressing. I knew quite well that she would violently oppose a second visit on my part to the deserted house down the street. I therefore, left a message for her that I had gone on, and, finding the street clear, met Sperry at his doorstep.

"This is the last sitting, Horace," he explained, "and I feel we ought to have the most complete possible knowledge, beforehand. We will be in a better position to understand what comes. There are two or three things we haven't checked up on."

He slipped an arm through mine, and we started down the street. "I'm going to get to the bottom of this, Horace, old dear," he said.

"Remember, we're pledged to a psychic investigation only."

"Rats!" he said rudely. "We are going to find out who killed Arthur Wells, and if he deserves hanging we'll hang him."

"Or her?"

"It wasn't Elinor Wells," he said positively. "Here's the point: if he's been afraid to go back for his overcoat it's still there. I don't expect that, however. But the thing about the curtain interests me. I've been reading over my copy of the notes on the sittings. It was said, you remember, that curtains—some curtains—would have been better places to hide the letters than the bag."

I stopped suddenly. "By jove, Sperry," I said. "I remember now. My notes of the sittings were in my overcoat."

"And they are gone?"

"They are gone."

He whistled softly. "That's unfortunate," he said. "Then the other person, whoever he is, knows what we know!"

He was considerably startled when I told him I had been shadowed, and insisted that it referred directly to the case in hand. "He's got your notes," he said, "and he's got to know what your next move is going to be."

His intention, I found, was to examine the carpet outside of the dressing-room door, and the floor beneath it, to discover if possible whether Arthur Wells had fallen there and been moved.

"Because I think you are right," he said. "He wouldn't have been likely to shoot himself in a hall, and because the very moving of the body would be in itself suspicious. Then I want to look at the curtains. 'The curtains would have been safer.' Safer for what? For the bag with the letters, probably, for she

220

followed that with the talk about Hawkins. He'd got them, and somebody was afraid he had."

"Just where does Hawkins come in, Sperry?" I asked.

"I'm damned if I know," he reflected. "We may learn tonight."

The Wells house was dark and forbidding. We walked past it once, as an officer was making his rounds in leisurely fashion, swinging his night-stick in circles. But on our return the street was empty, and we turned in at the side entry.

I led the way with comparative familiarity. It was, you will remember, my third similar excursion. With Sperry behind me I felt confident.

"In case the door is locked, I have a few skeleton keys," said Sperry.

We had reached the end of the narrow passage, and emerged into the square of brick and grass that lay behind the house. While the night was clear, the place lay in comparative darkness. Sperry stumbled over something, and muttered to himself.

The rear porch lay in deep shadow. We went up the steps together. Then Sperry stopped, and I advanced to the doorway. It was locked.

With my hand on the doorknob, I turned to Sperry. He was struggling violently with a dark figure, and even as I turned they went over with a crash and rolled together down the steps. Only one of them rose.

I was terrified. I confess it. It was impossible to see whether it was Sperry or his assailant. If it was Sperry who lay in a heap on the ground, I felt that I was lost. I could not escape. The way was blocked, and behind me the door, to which I now turned frantically, was a

221

barrier I could not move.

Then, out of the darkness behind me, came Sperry's familiar, booming bass. "I've knocked him out, I'm afraid. Got a match, Horace?"

Much shaken, I went down the steps and gave Sperry a wooden toothpick, under the impression that it was a match. That rectified, we bent over the figure on the bricks.

"Knocked out, for sure," said Sperry, "but I think it's not serious. A watchman, I suppose. Poor devil, we'll have to get him into the house."

The lock gave way to manipulation at last, and the door swung open. There came to us the heavy odor of all closed houses, a combination of carpets, cooked food, and floor wax. My nerves, now taxed to their utmost, fairly shrank from it, but Sperry was cool.

He bore the brunt of the weight as we carried the watchman in, holding him with his arms dangling, helpless and rather pathetic. Sperry glanced around. "Into the kitchen," he said. "We can lock him in."

We had hardly laid him on the floor when I heard the slow stride of the officer of the beat. He had turned into the paved alleyway, and was advancing with measured, ponderous steps. Fortunately I am an agile man, and thus I was able to get to the other door, reverse the key and turn it from the inside, before I heard him hailing the watchman.

"Hello there!" he called. "George, I say! George!"

He listened for a moment, then came up and tried the door. I crouched inside, as guilty as the veriest housebreaker in the business. But he had no suspicion, clearly, for he turned and went away, whistling as he went.

Not until we heard him going down the street again, absently running his night-stick along the fence palings, did Sperry or I move.

"A narrow squeak, that," I said, mopping my face.

"A miss is as good as a mile," he observed, and there was a sort of exultation in his voice. He is a born adventurer.

He came out into the passage and quickly locked the door behind him.

"Now, friend Horace," he said, "if you have anything but toothpicks for matches, we will look for the overcoat, and then we will go upstairs."

"Suppose he wakens and raises an alarm?"

"We'll be out of luck. That's all."

As we had anticipated, there was no overcoat in the library and, after listening a moment at the kitchen door, we ascended a rear staircase to the upper floor. I had, it will be remembered, fallen from a chair on a table in the dressing-room, and had left them thus overturned when I charged the third floor. The room, however, was now in perfect order, and when I held my candle to the ceiling, I perceived that the bullet hole had again been repaired, and this time with such skill that I could not even locate it.

"We are up against someone cleverer than we are, Sperry," I acknowledged.

"And who has more to lose than we have to gain," he added cheerfully. "Don't worry about that, Horace. You're a married man and I'm not. If a woman wanted to hide some letters from her husband, and chose a curtain for a receptacle, what room would she hide them in. Not in his dressing-room, eh?"

He took the candle and led the way to Elinor Wells's bedroom. Here, however, the draperies were down, and we would have been at a loss had I not remembered my wife's custom of folding draperies when we close the house, and placing them under the dusting sheets which cover the various beds.

Our inspection of the curtains was hurried, and broken by various excursions on my part to listen for the watchman. But he remained quiet below, and finally we found what we were looking for. In the lining of one of the curtains, near the bottom, a long, ragged cut had been made.

"Cut in a hurry, with curved scissors," was Sperry's comment. "Probably manicure scissors."

The result was a sort of pocket in the curtain, concealed on the chintz side, which was the side which would hang toward the room.

"Probably," he said, "the curtain *would* have been better. It would have stayed anyhow. Whereas the bag—" He was flushed with triumph. "How in the world would Hawkins know that?" he demanded. "You can talk all you like. She's told us things that no one ever told her."

Before examining the floor in the hall I went downstairs and listened outside the kitchen door. The watchman was stirring inside the room, and groaning occasionally. Sperry, however, when I told him, remained cool and in his exultant mood, and I saw that he meant to vindicate Miss Jeremy if he flung me into jail and the newspapers while doing it.

"We'll have a go at the floors under the carpets now," he said. "If he gets noisy, you can go down with the fire-tongs. I understand you are an expert with them."

The dressing-room had a large rug, like the nursery above it, and turning back the carpet was a simple matter. There had been a stain beneath where the dead man's head had lain, but it had been scrubbed and scraped away. The boards were white for an area of a square foot or so.

Sperry eyed the spot with indifference. "Not essential," he said. "Shows good housekeeping. That's all. The point is, are there other spots?"

And, after a time, we found what we were after. The upper hall was carpeted, and my penknife came into requisition to lift the tacks. They came up rather easily, as if but recently put in. That, indeed, proved to be the case.

Just outside the dressing-room door the boards for an area of two square feet or more beneath the carpet had been scraped and scrubbed. With the lifting of the carpet came, too, a strong odor, as of ammonia. But the stain of blood had absolutely disappeared.

Sperry, kneeling on the floor with the candle held close, examined the wood. "Not only scrubbed," he said, "but scraped down, probably with a floor-scraper. It's pretty clear, Horace. The poor devil fell here. There was a struggle, and he went down. He lay there for a while, too, until some plan was thought out. A man does not usually kill himself in a hallway. It's a sort of solitary deed. He fell here, and was dragged into the room. The angle of the bullet in the ceiling would probably show it came from here, too, and went through the doorway."

We were startled at that moment by a loud banging below. Sperry leaped to his feet and caught up his hat.

"The watchman," he said. "We'd better get out. He'll have all the neighbors in at that rate."

He was still hammering on the door as we went down the rear stairs, and Sperry stood outside the door and to one side.

"Keep out of range, Horace," he cautioned me. And to the watchman:

"Now, George, we will put the key under the door, and in ten minutes you may come out. Don't come sooner. I've warned you."

By the faint light from outside I could see him stooping, not in front of the door, but behind it. And it was well he did, for the moment the key was on the other side, a shot zipped through one of the lower panels. I had not expected it, and it set me to shivering.

"No more of that, George," said Sperry calmly and cheerfully. "This is a quiet neighborhood, and we don't like shooting. What is more, my friend here is very expert with his own particular weapon, and at any moment he may go to the fireplace in the library and—"

I have no idea why Sperry chose to be facetious at that time, and my resentment rises as I record it. For when we reached the yard we heard the officer running along the alleyway, calling as he ran.

"The fence, quick," Sperry said.

I am not very good at fences, as a rule, but I leaped that one like a cat, and came down in a barrel of wastepaper on the other side. Getting me out was a breathless matter, finally accomplished by turning the barrel over so that I could crawl out. We could hear the excited voices of the two men beyond the fence, and we ran. I was better than Sperry at that. I ran like a rabbit. I never even felt my legs. And Sperry pounded on behind me.

We heard, behind us, one of the men climbing the fence. But in jumping down he seemed to have struck the side of the overturned barrel. Probably it rolled and threw him, for that part of my mind which was not intent on flight heard him fall, and curse loudly.

"Go to it," Sperry panted behind me. "Roll over and break your neck." This, I need hardly explain, was meant for our pursuer.

We turned a corner and were out on one of the main thoroughfares. Instantly, so innate is cunning to the human brain, we fell to walking sedately.

It was as well that we did, for we had not gone a half block before we saw our policeman again, lumbering toward us and blowing a whistle as he ran.

"Stop and get this cab," Sperry directed me. "And don't breathe so hard."

The policeman stared at us fixedly, stopping to do so, but all he saw was two well-dressed and professional-looking men, one of them rather elderly, who was hailing a cab. I had the presence of mind to draw my watch and consult it.

"Just in good time," I said distinctly, and I entered the cab. Sperry remained on the curb and lighted a cigar. This gave him a chance to look back.

"Rather narrow squeak, that," he observed, as he sat down beside me. "Your gray hairs probably saved us."

I was quite numb from the waist down, from my

227

tumble and from running, and it was some time before I could breathe quietly. Suddenly Sperry fell to laughing.

"I wish you could have seen yourself in that barrel, and crawling out," he said.

We reached Mrs. Dane's, to find that Miss Jeremy had already arrived, looking rather pale, as I had noticed she always did before a seance. Her color had faded, and her eyes seemed sunken in her head.

"Not ill, are you?" Sperry asked her, as he took her hand.

"Not at all. But I am anxious. I always am. These things do not come for the calling."

"This is the last time. You have promised."

"Yes. The last time."

Chapter 10

It appeared that Herbert Robinson had been reading, during his convalescence, a considerable amount of psychic literature, and that we were to hold this third and final sitting under test conditions. As before, the room had been stripped of furniture, and the cloth and rod which formed the low screen behind Miss Jeremy's chair were not of her own providing, but Herbert's.

He had also provided, for some reason or other, eight small glass cups, into which he placed the legs of the two tables, and in a businesslike manner he set out on the large stand a piece of white paper, a pencil, and a spool of black thread. It is characteristic of Miss Jeremy, and of her own ignorance of the methods employed in professional seances, that she was as much interested and puzzled as we were.

When he had completed his preparations, Herbert made a brief speech.

"Members of the Neighborhood Club," he said impressively, "we have agreed among ourselves that this is to be our last meeting for the purpose that is before us. I have felt, therefore, that in justice to the medium this final seance should leave us with every conviction of its genuineness. Whatever phenomena occur, the medium must be, as she has been, above suspicion. For the replies of her 'control,' no particular precaution seems necessary, or possible. But the first seance divided itself into two parts: an early period when, so far as we could observe, the medium was at least partly conscious, possibly fully so, when physical demonstrations occurred. And a second, or trance period, during which we received replies to questions. It is for the physical phenomena that I am about to take certain precautions."

"Are you going to tie me?" Miss Jeremy asked.

"Do you object?"

"Not at all. But with what?"

"With silk thread," Herbert said, smilingly.

She held out her wrists at once, but Herbert placed her in her chair, and proceeded to wrap her, chair and all, in a strong network of fine threads, drawn sufficiently taut to snap with any movement.

He finished by placing her feet on the sheet of paper, and outlining their position there with a pencil line.

The proceedings were saved from absurdity by what we all felt was the extreme gravity of the situation. There were present in the room Mrs. Dane, the Robinsons, Sperry, my wife and myself, Clara, Mrs. Dane's secretary, had begged off on the plea of nervousness from the earlier and physical portion of the seance, and was to remain outside in the hall until the trance commenced.

Sperry objected to this, as movement in the circle during the trance had, in the first seance, induced fretful uneasiness in the medium. But Clara, appealed to, begged to be allowed to remain outside until she was required, and showed such unmistakable nervousness that we finally agreed.

"Would a slight noise disturb her?" Mrs. Dane asked.

Miss Jeremy thought not, if the circle remained unbroken, and Mrs. Dane considered.

"Bring me my stick from the hall, Horace," she said. "And tell Clara I'll rap on the floor with it when I want her."

I found a stick in the rack outside and brought it in. The lights were still on in the chandelier overhead, and as I gave the stick to Mrs. Dane I heard Sperry speaking sharply behind me.

"Where did you get that stick?" he demanded.

"In the hall. I—"

"I never saw it before," said Mrs. Dane. "Perhaps it is Herbert's."

But I caught Sperry's eye. We had both recognized it. It was Arthur Wells's, the one which Sperry had taken from his room, and which, in turn, had been taken from Sperry's library.

Sperry was watching me with a sort of cynical amusement. "You're an absent-minded beggar, Horace," he said.

"You didn't, by any chance, stop here on your way back from my place the other night, did you?"

"I did. But I didn't bring that thing."

"Look here, Horace," he said, more gently, "you come in and see me some day soon. You're not as fit as you ought to be."

I confess to a sort of helpless indignation that was far from the composure the occasion required. But the others, I believe, were fully convinced that no human agency had operated to bring the stick into Mrs. Dane's house, a belief that prepared them for anything that might occur.

A number of things occurred almost as soon as the lights were out, interrupting a train of thought in which I saw myself in the first stages of mental decay, and carrying about the streets not only fire-tongs and walking-sticks, but other portable property belonging to my friends.

Perhaps my excitement had a bad effect on the medium. She was uneasy and complained that the threads that bound her arms were tight. She was distinctly fretful. But after a time she settled down in her chair. Her figure, a deeper shadow in the semi-darkness of the room, seemed sagged—seemed, in some indefinable way, smaller. But there was none of the stertorous breathing that preceded trance.

Then, suddenly, a bell that Sperry had placed on the stand beyond the black curtain commenced to ring. It rang at first gently, then violently. It made a hideous clamor. I had a curious sense that it was ringing up in the air, near the top of the curtain. It was a relief to have it thrown to the ground, its racket silenced.

Quite without warning, immediately after, my chair twisted under me. "I am being turned around," I said in a low tone. "It is as if something has taken hold of the back of the chair and is twisting it. It has stopped now." I had been turned fully a quarter round.

For five minutes, by the luminous dial of my watch on the table before me, nothing further occurred, except that the black curtain appeared to swell, as in a wind.

"There is something behind it," Alice Robinson said, in a terrorized tone. "Something behind it, moving."

"It is not possible," Herbert assured her. "Nothing, that is—there is only one door, and it is closed. I have examined the walls and floor carefully."

At the end of five minutes something soft and fragrant fell onto the table near me. I had not noticed Herbert when he placed the flowers from Mrs. Dane's table on the stand, and I was more startled than the others. Then the glass prisms in the chandelier over our heads clinked together, as if they had been swept by a finger. More of the flowers came. We were pelted with them. And into the quiet that followed there came a light, fine but steady tattoo on the table in our midst. Then at last silence, and the medium in deep trance, and Mrs. Dane rapping on the floor for Clara.

When Clara came in, Mrs. Dane told her to switch on the lights. Miss Jeremy had dropped in her chair until the silk across her chest was held taut. But investigation showed that none of the threads were broken and that her evening slippers still fitted into the outline on the paper beneath them. Without getting up, Sperry reached to the stand behind Miss Jeremy, and brought into view a piece of sculptor's clay he had placed there. The handle of the bell was now jammed into the mass. He had only time to show it to us when the medium began to speak.

I find, on re-reading the earlier part of this record, that I have omitted mention of Miss Jeremy's "control." So suddenly had we jumped, that first evening, into the trail that led us to the Wells case, that beyond the rather raucous "good-evening," and possibly the extraneous matter referring to Mother Goose and so on, we had been saved the usual preliminary patter of the average control.

On this night, however, we were obliged to sit impatiently through a rambling discourse, given in a half-belligerent manner, on the deterioration of moral standards. Re-reading Clara's notes, I find that the subject matter is without originality and the diction inferior. But the lecture ceased abruptly, and the time for questions had come.

"Now," Herbert said, "we want you to go back to the house where you saw the dead man on the floor. You know his name, don't you?"

There was a pause. "Yes. Of course I do. A. L. Wells."

Arthur had been known to most of us by his Christian name, but the initials were correct.

"How do you know it is an L?"

"On letters," was the laconic answer. Then: "Letters, letters, who has the letters?"

"Do you know whose cane this is?"

"Yes."

"Will you tell us?"

Up to that time the replies had come easily and quickly. But beginning with the cane question, the medium was in difficulties. She moved uneasily, and spoke irritably. The replies were slow and grudging. Foreign subjects were introduced, as now.

"Horace's wife certainly bullies him," said the voice. "He's afraid of her. And the fire-tongs—the fire-tongs—the fire-tongs!"

"Whose cane is this?" Herbert repeated.

"Mr. Ellingham's."

This created a profound sensation.

"How do you know that?"

"He carried at at the seashore. He wrote in the sand with it."

"What did he write?"

"Ten o'clock."

"He wrote 'ten o'clock' in the sand, and the waves came and washed it away?"

"Yes."

"Horace," said my wife, leaning forward, "why not ask her about that stock of mine? If it is going down, I ought to sell, oughtn't I?"

Herbert eyed her with some exasperation.

"We are here to make a serious investigation," he said. "If the members of the club will keep their attention on what we are doing, we may get somewhere. Now," to the medium, "the man is dead, and the revolver is beside him. Did he kill himself?"

"No. He attacked her when he found the letters."

"And she shot him?"

"I can't tell you that."

"Try very hard. It is important."

"I don't know," was the fretful reply. "She may have. She hated him. I don't know. She says she did."

"She says she killed him?"

But there was no reply to this, although Herbert repeated it several times.

Instead the voice of the "control" began to recite a

verse of poetry—a cheap, sentimental bit of trash. It was maddening, under the circumstances.

"Do you know where the letters are?"

"Hawkins has them."

"They were not hidden in the curtain?" This was Sperry.

"No. The police might have searched the room."

"Where were these letters?"

There was no direct reply to this but instead: "He found them when he was looking for his razorstrop. They were in the top of a closet. His revolver was there, too. He went back and got it. It was terrible."

There was a profound silence, followed by a slight exclamation from Sperry as he leaped to his feet. The screen at the end of the room, which cut off the light from Clara's candle, was toppling. The next instant it fell, and we saw Clara sprawled over her table, in a dead faint.

Chapter 11

In this, the final chapter of the record of these seances, I shall give, as briefly as possible, the events of the day following the third sitting. I shall explain the mystery of Arthur Wells's death, and I shall give the solution arrived at by the Neighborhood Club as to the strange communications from the medium, Miss Jeremy, now Sperry's wife.

But there are some things I cannot explain. Do our spirits live on, on this earth plane, now and then obedient to the wills of those yet living? Is death, then, only a gateway into higher space, from which, through the open door of a "sensitive" mind, we may be brought back on occasion to commit the inadequate absurdities of the physical seance?

Or is Sperry right, and do certain individuals manifest powers of a purely physical nature, but powers which Sperry characterizes as the survival of some long-lost development by which at one time we knew how to liberate a forgotten form of energy?

Who can say? We do not know. We have had to

accept these things as they have been accepted through the ages, and give them either a spirtual or a purely natural explanation, as our minds happen to be adventurous or analytic in type.

But outside of the purely physical phenomena of those seances, we are provided with an explanation which satisfies the Neighborhood Club, even if it fails to satisfy the convinced spiritist. We have been accused merely of substituting one mystery for another, but I reply by saying that the mystery we substitute is not a mystery, but an acknowledged fact.

On Tuesday morning I wakened after an uneasy night. I knew certain things, knew them definitely in the clear light of morning. Hawkins had the letters that Arthur Wells had found; that was one thing. I had not taken Ellingham's stick to Mrs. Dane's house; that was another. I had not done it. I had placed it on the table and had not touched it again.

But those were immaterial, compared with one outstanding fact. Any supernatural solution would imply full knowledge by whatever power had controlled the medium. And there was not full knowledge. There was, on the contrary, a definite place beyond which the medium could not go.

She did not know who had killed Arthur Wells.

To my surprise, Sperry and Herbert Robinson came together to see me that morning at my office. Sperry, like myself, was pale and tired, but Herbert was restless and talkative, for all the world like a terrier on the scent of a rat.

They had brought a newspaper account of an attempt by burglars to rob the Wells house, and the usual police formula that arrests were expected to be made that day. There was a diagram of the house, and a picture of the kitchen door, with an arrow indicating the bullet hole.

"Hawkins will be here soon," Sperry said, rather casually, after I had read the clipping.

"Here?"

"Yes. He is bringing a letter from Miss Jeremy. The letter is merely a blind. We want to see him."

Herbert was examining the door of my office. He set the spring lock. "He may try to bolt," he explained. "We're in this pretty deep, you know."

"How about a record of what he says?" Sperry asked.

I pressed a button, and Miss Joyce came in. "Take the testimony of the man who is coming in, Miss Joyce," I directed. "Take everything we say, any of us. Can you tell the different voices?"

She thought she could, and took up her position in the next room, with the door partly open.

I can still see Hawkins as Sperry let him in—a tall, cadaverous man of good manners and an English accent, a superior servant. He was cool but rather resentful. I judged that he considered carrying letters as in no way a part of his work, and that he was careful of his dignity.

"Miss Jeremy sent this, sir," he said.

Then his eyes took in Sperry and Herbert, and he drew himself up.

"I see," he said. "It wasn't the letter, then?"

"Not entirely. We want to have a talk with you, Hawkins."

"Very well, sir." But his eyes went from one to the other of us.

"You were in the employ of Mr. Wells. We know that. Also we saw you there the night he died, but some time after his death. What time did you get in that night?"

"About midnight. I am not certain."

"Who told you of what had happened?"

"I told you that before. I met the detectives going out."

"Exactly. Now, Hawkins, you had come in, locked the door, and placed the key outside for the other servants?"

"Yes, sir."

"How do you expect us to believe that?" Sperry demanded irritably. "There was only one key. Could you lock yourself in and then place the key outside?"

"Yes, sir," he replied impassively. "By opening the kitchen window, I could reach out and hang it on the nail."

"You were out of the house, then, at the time Mr. Wells died?"

"I can prove it by as many witnesses as you wish to call."

"Now, about these letters, Hawkins," Sperry said. "The letters in the bag. Have you still got them?"

He half rose—we had given him a chair facing the light—and then sat down again. "What letters?"

"Don't beat about the bush. We know you have the letters. And we want them."

"I don't intend to give them up, sir."

"Will you tell us how you got them?"

He hesitated. "If you do not know already, I do not care to say."

I placed the letter to A 31 before him. "You wrote

240

this, I think?" I said.

He was genuinely startled. More than that, indeed, for his face twitched. "Suppose I did?" he said. "I'm not admitting it."

"Will you tell us for whom it was meant?"

"You know a great deal already, gentlemen. Why not find that out from where you learned the rest?"

"You know, then, where we learned what we know?"

"That's easy," he said bitterly. "She's told you enough, I dare say. She doesn't know it all, of course. Any more than I do," he added.

"Will you give us the letters?"

"I haven't said I have them. I haven't admitted I wrote that one on the desk. Suppose I have them, I'll not give them up except to the District Attorney."

"By 'she' do you refer to Miss Jeremy?" I asked.

He stared at me, and then smiled faintly.

"You know who I mean."

We tried to assure him that we were not, in a sense, seeking to involve him in the situation, and I even went so far as to state our position, briefly:

"I'd better explain, Hawkins. We are not doing police work. But, owing to a chain of circumstances, we have learned that Mr. Wells did not kill himself. He was murdered, or at least shot by someone else. It may not have been deliberate. Owing to what we have learned, certain people are under suspicion. We want to clear things up for our own satisfaction."

"Then why is someone taking down what I say in the next room?"

He could only have guessed it, but he saw that he was right, by our faces. He smiled bitterly. "Go on," he said. "Take it down. It can't hurt anybody. I don't know who did it, and that's God's truth."

And, after long wrangling, that was as far as we got.

He suspected who had done it, but he did not know. He absolutely refused to surrender the letters in his possession, and a sense of delicacy, I think, kept us all from pressing the question of the A 31 matter.

"That's a personal affair," he said. "I've had a good bit of trouble. I'm thinking now of going back to England."

And, as I say, we did not insist.

When he had gone, there seemed to be nothing to say. He had left the same impression on all of us, I think—of trouble, but not of crime. Of a man fairly driven; of wretchedness that was almost despair. He still had the letters. He had, after all, as much right to them as we had, which was, actually, not right at all. And, whatever it was, he still had his secret.

Herbert was almost childishly crestfallen. Sperry's attitude was more philosophical.

"A woman, of course," he said. "The A 31 letter shows it. He tried to get her back, perhaps, by holding the letters over her head. And it hasn't worked out. Poor devil! Only—who is the woman?"

It was that night, the fifteenth day after the crime, that the solution came. Came, as a matter of fact, to my door.

I was in the library, reading, or trying to read, a rather abstruse book on psychic phenomena, when the bell rang.

In our modest establishment the maids retire early,

and it is my custom, on those rare occasions when the bell rings after nine o'clock, to answer the door myself.

To my surprise, it was Sperry, accompanied by two ladies, one of them heavily veiled. It was not until I had ushered them into the reception room that I saw who they were. It was Elinor Wells, in deep mourning, and Clara, Mrs. Dane's companion and secretary.

I am afraid I was rather excited, for I took Sperry's hat from him and placed it on the head of a marble bust which I had given my wife on our last anniversary, and Sperry says that I drew a smoking-stand up beside Elinor Wells with great care. I do not know. It has, however, passed into history in the Club, where every now and then for some time Herbert offered one of the ladies a cigar, with my compliments.

My wife, I believe, was advancing along the corridor when Sperry closed the door. As she had only had time to see that a woman was in the room, she was naturally resentful, and retired to the upper floor, where I found her considerably upset, some time later.

While I am quite sure that I was not thinking clearly at the opening of the interview, I know that I was puzzled at the presence of Mrs. Dane's secretary, but I doubtless accepted it as having some connection with Clara's notes. And Sperry, at the beginning, made no comment on her at all.

"Mrs. Wells suggested that we come here, Horace," he began. "We may need a legal mind on this. I'm not sure, or rather I think it unlikely. But just in case—

243

suppose you tell him, Elinor.''

I have no record of the story Elinor Wells told that night in our little reception-room, with Clara sitting in a corner, grave and white. It was fragmentary, incoordinate. But I got it all at last.

Charlie Ellingham had killed Arthur Wells, but in a struggle. In parts the story was sordid enough. She did not spare herself, or her motives. She had wanted luxury, and Arthur had not succeeded as he had promised. They were in debt, and living beyond their means. But even that, she hastened to add, would not have mattered, had he not been brutal with her. He had made her life very wretched.

But on the subject of Charlie Ellingham she was emphatic. She knew that there had been talk, but there had been no real basis for it. She had turned to him for comfort, and he gave her love. She didn't know where he was now, and didn't greatly care, but she would like to recover and destroy some letters he had written her.

She was looking crushed and ill, and she told her story inco-ordinately and nervously. Reduced to its elements, it was as follows:

On the night of Arthur Wells's death they were dressing for a ball. She had made a private arrangement with Ellingham to plead a headache at the last moment and let Arthur go alone. But he had been so insistent that she had been forced to go, after all. She had sent the governess, Suzanne Gautier, out to telephone Ellingham not to come, but he was not at his house, and the message was left with his valet. As it turned out, he had already started.

Elinor was dressed, all but her ball-gown, and had

put on a negligée, to wait for the governess to return and help her. Arthur was in his dressing-room, and she heard him grumbling about having no blades for his safety razor.

He got out a case of razors and searched for the strop. When she remembered where the strop was, it was too late. The letters had been beside it, and he was coming toward her, with them in his hand.

She was terrified. He had read only one, but that was enough. He muttered something and turned away. She saw his face as he went toward where the revolver had been hidden from the children, and she screamed.

Charlie Ellingham heard her. The door had been left unlocked by the governess, and he was in the lower hall. He ran up and the two men grappled. The first shot was fired by Arthur. It struck the ceiling. The second she was doubtful about. She thought the revolver was still in Arthur's hand. It was all horrible. He went down like a stone, in the hallway outside the door.

They were nearly mad, the two of them. They had dragged the body in, and then faced each other. Ellingham was for calling the police at once and surrendering, but she had kept him away from the telephone. She maintained, and I think it very possible, that her whole thought was for the children, and the effect on their after lives of such a scandal. And, after all, nothing could help the man on the floor.

It was while they were trying to formulate some concerted plan that they heard footsteps below and, thinking it was Mademoiselle Gautier, she drove

Ellingham into the rear of the house, from which later he managed to escape. But it was Clara who was coming up the stairs.

"She had been our first governess for the children," Elinor said, "and she often came in. She had made a birthday smock for Buddy, and she had it in her hand. She almost fainted. I couldn't tell her about Charlie Ellingham. I couldn't. I told her we had been struggling, and that I was afraid I had shot him. She is quick. She knew just what to do. We worked fast. She said a suicide would not have fired one shot into the ceiling, and she fixed that. It was terrible. And all the time he lay there, with his eyes half open—"

The letters, it seems, were all over the place. Elinor thought of the curtain, cut a receptacle for them, but she was afraid of the police. Finally she gave them to Clara, who was to take them away and burn them.

They did everything they could think of, all the time listening for Suzanne Gautier's return; filled the second empty chamber of the revolver, dragged the body out of the hall and washed the carpet, and called Doctor Sperry, knowing that he was at Mrs. Dane's and could not come.

Clara had only a little time, and with the letters in her handbag she started down the stairs. There she heard someone, possibly Ellingham, on the back stairs, and in her haste she fell, hurting her knee, and she must have dropped the handbag at that time. They knew now that Hawkins had found it later on. But for a few days they didn't know, and hence the advertisement.

"I think we would better explain Hawkins," Sperry said. "Hawkins was married to Miss Clara here, some years ago, while she was with Mrs. Wells. They kept it a secret, and recently she has broken with him."

"He was infatuated with another woman," Clara said briefly. "That's a personal matter. It has nothing to do with this case."

"It explains Hawkins's letter."

"It doesn't explain how that medium knew everything that happened," Clara put in, excitedly. "She knew it all, even the library paste! I can tell you Mr. Johnson, I was close to fainting a dozen times before I finally did it."

"Did you know of our seances?" I asked Mrs. Wells.

"Yes. I may as well tell you that I haven't been in Florida. How could I? The children are there, but I—"

"Did you tell Charlie Ellingham about them?"

"After the second one I warned him, and I think he went to the house. One bullet was somewhere in the ceiling, or in the floor of the nursery. I thought it ought to be found. I don't know whether he found it or not. I've been afraid to see him."

She sat, clasping and unclasping her hands in her lap. She was a proud woman, and surrender had come hard. The struggle was marked in her face. She looked as though she had not slept for days.

"You think I am frightened," she said slowly. "And I am, terribly frightened. But not about discovery. That has come, and cannot be helped."

"Then why?"

"How does this woman, this medium, know these things?" Her voice rose, with an unexpected hysteri-

247

cal catch. "It is superhuman. I am almost mad."

"We're going to get to the bottom of this," Sperry said soothingly. "Be sure that it is not what you think it is, Elinor. There's a simple explanation, and I think I've got it. What about the stick that was taken from my library?"

"Will you tell me how you came to have it, doctor?"

"Yes. I took it from the lower hall the night—the night it happened."

"It was Charlie Ellingham's. He had left it there. We had to have it, doctor. Alone it might not mean much, but with the other things you knew—tell them, Clara."

"I stole it from your office," Clara said, looking straight ahead. "We had to have it. I knew at the second sitting that it was his."

"When did you take it?"

"On Monday morning, I went for Mrs. Dane's medicine, and you had promised her a book. Do you remember? I told your man, and he allowed me to go up to the library. It was there, on the table. I had expected to have to search for it, but it was lying out. I fastened it to my belt, under my long coat."

"And placed it in the rack at Mrs. Dane's?" Sperry was watching her intently, with the same sort of grim intentness he wears when examining a chest.

"I put it in the closet in my room. I meant to get rid of it, when I had a little time. I don't know how it got downstairs, but I think—"

"Yes?"

"We are house-cleaning. A housemaid was washing closets. I suppose she found it and, thinking it was one of Mrs. Dane's, took it downstairs. That is, unless—" It was clear that, like Elinor, she had a supernatural explanation in her mind. She looked gaunt and haggard.

"Mr. Ellingham was anxious to get it," she finished. "He had taken Mr. Johnson's overcoat by mistake one night when you were both in the house, and the notes were in it. He saw that the stick was important."

"Clara," Sperry asked, "did you see, the day you advertised for your bag, another similar advertisement?"

"I saw it. It frightened me."

"You have no idea who inserted it?"

"None whatever."

"Did you ever see Miss Jeremy before the first sitting? Or hear of her?"

"Never."

"Or between the seances?"

"No."

Elinor rose and drew her veil down. "We must go," she said. "Surely now you will cease these terrible investigations. I cannot stand much more. I am going mad."

"There will be no more seances," Sperry said gravely.

"What are you going to do?" She turned to me, I dare say because I represented what to her was her supreme dread, the law.

"My dear girl," I said, "we are not going to do anything. The Neighborhood Club has been doing a little amateur research work, which is now over. That is all."

Sperry took them away in his car, but he turned on the doorstep, "Wait downstairs for me," he said, "I am coming back."

I remained in the library until he returned, uneasily pacing the floor.

For where were we, after all? We had had the medium's story elaborated and confirmed, but the fact remained that, step by step, through her unknown "control" the Neighborhood Club had followed a tragedy from its beginning, or almost its beginning, to its end.

Was everything on which I had built my life to go? Its philosophy, its science, even its theology, before the revelations of a young woman who knew hardly the rudiments of the very things she was destroying?

Was death, then, not peace and an awakening to new things, but a wretched and dissociated clutching after the old? A wrench which only loosened but did not break our earthly ties?

It was well that Sperry came back when he did, bringing with him a breath of fresh night air and stalwart sanity. He found me still pacing the room.

"The thing I want to know," I said fretfully, "is where this leaves us? Where are we? For God's sake, where are we?"

"Well," said Sperry, "so you want to know where we are?"

"I would like to save something out of the wreck."

"That's easy. Horace, you should be a heart specialist, and I should have taken the law. It's as plain as the alphabet." He took his notes of the sittings from his pocket. "I'm going to read a few things. Keep what is left of your mind on them. This

250

is the first sitting.

"'The knee hurts. It is very bad. Arnica will take the pain out.'

"'I want to go out. I want air. If I could only go to sleep and forget it. The drawing-room furniture is scattered all over the house.'

"Now the second sitting:

"'It is writing.' (The stick.) 'It is writing, but the water washed it away. All of it, not a trace.' 'If only the pocketbook were not lost. Car-tickets and letters. It will be terrible if the letters are found.' 'Hawkins may have it. The curtain was much safer.' 'That part's safe enough, unless it made a hole in the floor above.'"

"Oh, if you're going to read a lot of irrelevant material—"

"Irrelevant nothing! Wake up, Horace! But remember this. I'm not explaining the physical phenomena. We'll never do that. It wasn't extraordinary, as such things go. Our little medium in a trance condition has read poor Clara's mind. It's all here, all that Clara knew and nothing that she didn't know. A mind-reader, friend Horace. And Heaven help me when I marry her!"

As I have said, the Neighborhood Club ended its investigations with this conclusion, which I believe is properly reached. It is only fair to state that there are those among us who have accepted that theory in the Wells case, but who have preferred to consider that behind both it and the physical phenomena of the seances there was an intelligence which directed both, an intelligence not of this world as we know it. Both Herbert and Alice Robinson are now pronounced spiritualists, although Miss Jeremy, now Mrs. Sperry, has definitely abandoned all investigative work.

Personally, I have evolved no theory. It seems beyond dispute that certain individuals can read minds, and that these same, or other so-called "sensitives," are capable of liberating a form of invisible energy which, however, they turn to no further account than the useless ringing of bells, moving of small tables, and flinging about of divers objects.

To me, I admit, the solution of the Wells case as one of mind-reading is more satisfactory than explanatory. For mental waves remain a mystery, acknowledged, as is electricity, but of a nature yet unrevealed. Thoughts are things. That is all we know.

Mrs. Dane, I believe, had suspected the solution from the start.

The Neighborhood Club has recently disbanded. We tried other things, but we had been spoiled. Our Kipling winter was a failure. We read a play or two, with Sperry's wife reading the heroine, and the rest of us taking other parts. She has a lovely voice, has Mrs. Sperry. But it was all stale and unprofitable, after the Wells affair. With Herbert on a lecture tour on spirit realism, and Mrs. Dane at a sanatorium for the winter, we have now given it up, and my wife and I spend our Monday evenings at home.

After dinner I read, or, as lately, I have been making this record of the Wells case from our notes.

My wife is still fond of the phonograph, and even now, as I make this last entry and complete my narrative, she is waiting for me to change the record. I will be frank. I hate the phonograph. I hope it will be destroyed, or stolen. I am thinking very seriously of having it stolen.

"Horace," says my wife, "whatever would we do without the phonograph? I wish you would put it in the burglar-insurance policy. I am always afraid it will be stolen."

Even here, you see! Truly thoughts are things.

MYSTERIES TO KEEP YOU GUESSING
by John Dickson Carr

CASTLE SKULL   (1974, $3.50)
The hand may be quicker than the eye, but ghost stories didn't hoodwink Henri Bencolin. A very real murderer was afoot in Castle Skull—a murderer who must be found before he strikes again.

IT WALKS BY NIGHT   (1931, $3.50)
The police burst in and found the Duc's severed head staring at them from the center of the room. Both the doors had been guarded, yet the murderer had gone in and out *without having been seen*!

THE EIGHT OF SWORDS   (1881, $3.50)
The evidence showed that while waiting to kill Mr. Depping, the murderer had calmly eaten his victim's dinner. But before famed crime-solver Dr. Gideon Fell could serve up the killer to Scotland Yard, there would be another course of murder.

THE MAN WHO COULD NOT SHUDDER (1703, $3.50)
Three guests at Martin Clarke's weekend party swore they saw the pistol lifted from the wall, levelled, and shot. *Yet no hand held it*. It couldn't have happened—but there was a dead body on the floor to prove that it had.

THE PROBLEM OF THE WIRE CAGE   (1702, $3.50)
There was only one set of footsteps in the soft clay surface—and those footsteps belonged to the victim. It seemed impossible to prove that anyone had killed Frank Dorrance.

THE BESTSELLING NOVELS
BEHIND THE BLOCKBUSTER MOVIES —
ZEBRA'S MOVIE MYSTERY GREATS!

HIGH SIERRA   (2059, $3.50)
by W.R. Burnett
A dangerous criminal on the lam is trapped in a terrifying web of circumstance. The tension-packed novel that inspired the 1955 film classic starring Humphrey Bogart and directed by John Houston.

MR. ARKADIN   (2145, $3.50)
by Orson Welles
A playboy's search to uncover the secrets of financier Gregory Arkadin's hidden past exposes a worldwide intrigue of big money, corruption — and murder. Orson Welles's only novel, and the basis for the acclaimed film written by, directed by, and starring himself.

NOBODY LIVES FOREVER   (2217, $3.50)
by W.R. Burnett
Jim Farrar's con game backfires when his beautiful victim lures him into a dangerous deception that could only end in death. A 1946 cinema classic starring John Garfield and Geraldine Fitzgerald. (AVAILABLE IN FEBRUARY 1988)

BUILD MY GALLOWS HIGH   (2341, $3.50)
by Geoffrey Homes
When Red Bailey's former lover Mumsie McGonigle lured him from the Nevada hills back to the deadly hustle of New York City, the last thing the ex-detective expected was to be set up as a patsy and framed for a murder he didn't commit. The novel that inspired the screen gem OUT OF THE PAST, starring Robert Mitchum and Kirk Douglas. (AVAILABLE IN APRIL 1988)

Available wherever paperbacks are sold, or order direct from the Publisher. Send cover price plus 50¢ per copy for mailing and handling to Zebra Books, Dept. 2707, 475 Park Avenue South, New York, N.Y. 10016. Residents of New York, New Jersey and Pennsylvania must include sales tax. DO NOT SEND CASH.

THE FINEST IN SUSPENSE!

THE URSA ULTIMATUM   (2130, $3.95)
by Terry Baxter
In the dead of night, twelve nuclear warheads are smuggled north across the Mexican border to be detonated simultaneously in major cities throughout the U.S. And only a small-town desert lawman stands between a face-less Russian superspy and World War Three!

THE LAST ASSASSIN   (1989, $3.95)
by Daniel Easterman
From New York City to the Middle East, the devastating flames of revolution and terrorism sweep across a world gone mad . . . as the most terrifying conspiracy in the history of mankind is born!

FLOWERS FROM BERLIN   (2060, $4.50)
by Noel Hynd
With the Earth on the brink of World War Two, the Third Reich's deadliest professional killer is dispatched on the most heinous assignment of his murderous career: the assassination of Franklin Delano Roosevelt!

THE BIG NEEDLE   (1921, $2.95)
by Ken Follett
All across Europe, innocent people are being terrorized, homes are destroyed, and dead bodies have become an unnervingly common sight. And the horrors will continue until the most powerful organization on Earth finds Chadwell Carstairs—and kills him!

DOMINATOR   (2118, $3.95)
by James Follett
Two extraordinary men, each driven by dangerously ambiguous loyalties, play out the ultimate nuclear endgame miles above the helpless planet—aboard a hijacked space shuttle called DOMINATOR!